SATAN and the PRIME MINISTER

by

Richard Asner

DORRANCE
PUBLISHING CO
EST. 1920
PITTSBURGH, PENNSYLVANIA 15238

Dorrance Publishing Co
585 Alpha Drive
Suite 103
Pittsburgh, PA 15238
Visit our website at *www.dorrancebookstore.com*

ISBN: 978-1-6470-2270-9
eISBN: 978-1-6470-2838-1

Chapter One

Saturday – March 3, 2018

5:10 P.M. Roman and Rina have just checked into Hotel Innsbrook in anticipation of getting in several days of skiing. After freshening up a bit, they head for the bar.

"Well, Rina, it's about time we got in the skiing we've been talking about for the past year. What would you like to drink, my dear?"

"I think I'll have something different tonight. I feel like a Mai Tai!"

"And you're hoping he'll top it off with a little umbrella!"

"I didn't say that!"

"I can read your mind, sweetheart!"

"Oh, you can, can you? Then what am I thinking now?"

"You are thinking little pink umbrellas!"

"I'm thinking I can't believe what I'm seeing! Am I really seeing things? Who do you see sitting by himself in a booth over there by a far wall?"

"I'm with you; it can't possibly be, but there is no denying it. It is either Mahmud Abuzar or his twin brother. What on earth is he doing here? Do you actually think he has taken up skiing? He has to be as much out of place as a member of the Cuban Olympic luge team. I don't think he has seen us. Let's go over and pay him a visit."

Mahmud glances up with a startled look of complete surprise as Roman and Rina approach his table. Roman leads off. "I can't tell you what a complete surprise this is to see you here in Innsbrook, the skiing capital of the world. How long have you been skiing?"

"I have to say, the feeling is mutual. I never thought I'd ever see the two of you again; however, I'm willing to let bygones be bygones if you are."

Roman looks at Rina. "I think that is probably a very good idea, at least for the moment."

Mahmud then offers, "Would you care to sit down?"

Roman and Rina both respond, "Thank you, Mahmud!"

The air is rather heavy and tense as the three try to make the best of what has turned out to be a very awkward moment. Roman sees that Mahmud's drink is almost empty and offers, "Let me buy you a refill, Mahmud!"

"I'm having a dry vodka martini, thank you!" Roman signals to the roving bar attendant. "Two dry vodka martinis and one Mai Tai, please!" Roman continues, "How long have you been skiing, Mahmud?"

"I took it up my first year in the States. I had time on my hands, and it looked like fun. I learned a lot with my time in the States. I guess I should be grateful to the both of you for banning me to live there. Life was quite restrictive living in Iran."

Roman asks, "Do you remember Ibrahim Zuwabi?"

"Yes, I remember him. You helped him escape from Iran with records of our nuclear weapons production."

"Did you know he became a professor at MIT specializing in laser technology?"

"Yes, I heard that!"

"Did you also know that he died as a result of a gun fight in a Moscow hotel?"

"No, I didn't know that. What was he doing in a Moscow hotel?"

"The reason for that, I'm afraid, will have to remain classified, but the one item that tortured him the moment he left Iran was the fate of his family. Can you possibly tell me where they are or what happened to them?"

"After Ibrahim's escape, his family was sent to serve life sentences in Evin Prison for his crime. While serving their second year, I hesitate to say, they were all shot trying to escape."

Roman and Rina pause for a moment, looking at one another and not saying a word, knowing that this was not the place nor the time. Any recriminations or acts of retribution would have to wait 'til later.

Mahmud breaks the silence by saying, "I can tell from your faces that you would like to take their fate out on me. I assure you, I had nothing to do with their capture or their sentence. That was strictly a police action."

"Tell me, Mahmud, do you know if their escape and death was a set-up?"

"I honestly don't know!"

Roman turns to Rina. "The one good thing we can say that came out of their deaths is perhaps now Ibrahim can finally be with his family up there somewhere in Allah's kingdom."

At this point, Roman and Rina get up as Roman says, "Rina and I will be getting up early tomorrow to hit the slopes. Maybe we may see you. Good night, Mahmud!"

· · · · ·

9:40 P.M. Mahmud is in his room, sitting at his desk, and wondering, *What is the best way to get rid of those two? They have been a constant thorn in my side for years. What can I do with my 9mm Luger? It would be better if I had a good rifle, but I don't have one. This Luger will have to do. Tomorrow I won't take the gondola to the last stop on top. I'll get off halfway up, pick out a good spot to hide, and wait for them as they ski back down. Wish I had a good rifle!*

Sunday – March 4, 2018

9:18 A.M. Roman and Rina see Mahmud in the midst of a large group of people waiting to board the gondola that just arrived. They wave and call over to

Mahmud. As they meet, Rina remarks, "Mahmud, never in my wildest dreams would I ever have believed that we be meeting like this preparing to board a skiing gondola in Innsbrook. Are you taking it to the top?"

"No, actually, I'm getting off about halfway up and trying the mogul run."

Rina responds, "Please, don't tell me you are a mogul skier!"

"I've tried the mogul slopes a few times. It's quite challenging!"

Roman chimes in, "Mahmud, you never cease to amaze me!"

About halfway up, Mahmud gets off, as both Roman and Rina say, "Good luck, Mahmud! We hope you make it down in one piece."

Mahmud waves good-bye, watches the gondola continue out of sight, and then begins to look for a good place to hide and watch as Roman and Rina take their normal run from the top of the mountain.

This looks like a good spot. I can crouch low behind this pile of snow that appears to be ideally located close enough to the run, yet far enough not to get noticed.

Time seems to crawl by as Mahmud waits for his prey. *Where are they? It's been over a half an hour.* Finally, Mahmud sees them in the distance. He holds his Luger in his right hand with the safety off, loaded, cocked and ready to fire. They are within range now. Mahmud takes aim and gets off two shots, one for each victim. Both shots miss and all Mahmud can do is watch as Roman and Rina whiz by.

Roman yells to Rina, "I think I heard what sounded like couple of shots being fired, and if I know my guns, they had the sound of a Luger."

Rina responds, "Do you think those shots were meant for us?"

"I don't see anyone else around! I think I need a drink."

When they reach the mountain base, Roman and Rina head for the nearby lodge and a waiting bar. They grab a booth, order their drinks, and begin talking about what happened on their run only to see Mahmud enter the bar. Roman signals and calls over to Mahmud to join them and then orders a dry vodka martini for Mahmud from the roving bar attendant.

Looking Mahmud squarely in the eye, Roman remarks, "You can't guess what happened to Rina and me on our run today. We both heard two shots from what sounded like a 9mm Luger at close range. You could almost say they were meant for us. Mahmud, who do you suppose would be shooting at us out here, apart from everyone in the world, but the avid ski enthusiast?"

"That is strange! I can't hazard a guess. Are you sure of what you heard?"

Roman responds, "Well, it sure wasn't the backfire from some antique automobile. They sounded like the shots from a 9mm Luger."

"You know the sound of a 9mm Luger?"

"Yes, I used to carry one during the eight years I worked for America's FBI."

"I guess then you ought to know! If you'll excuse me now, I'm going to my room to freshen up a bit. Maybe I'll see you at dinner."

Monday – March 5, 2018

10:18 A.M. Just as the day before, Mahmud has left the gondola halfway up to the top on the pretense of trying the mogul run one more time. He is occupying the same spot, crouched low behind the same snowbank.

Roman and Rina have reached the top of the mountain and are putting on their skis. Roman remarks, "Mahmud got off at the same spot as yesterday. You know he'll be waiting for us at the same place. We'll have to be ready for him. Keep your eye on me; when we reach about ten yards before the spot when we heard the shots yesterday, abruptly stop and crouch low. As we approach, he'll start firing. Spot where the shots are coming from and start firing back with all you've got. When and if he runs out of ammo, he'll start off skiing as fast as he can. I doubt if he is prepared with many shells. Under the circumstances, he probably doesn't see the need. Okay, Rina, remember what I told you. Let's go!"

The run down is fairly swift and as they approach the spot, Roman signals! They break to an abrupt stop and crouch down.

Mahmud is caught by surprise and begins shooting in their direction. Then Roman points in the direction of the fire and both begin to empty their pistols toward Mahmud's snowbank.

As predicted, Mahmud has spent his last round and begins to frantically ski down the run. Mahmud becomes exceedingly harried and flustered as he looks back and sees Roman and Rina right on his tail. He skis as fast as his ability will take him as he continues to look back and see Roman and Rina right behind him. But in looking back, Mahmud becomes disoriented and veers off the normal run onto ungroomed, pristine snow. Now he has no idea where he is.

Roman and Rina watch him as he unknowingly reaches the edge of a cliff, skis off into the air, and falls a thousand feet to his death.

Roman and Rina look at one another as if to say in a somewhat woeful way, "Well, sweetheart, this closes another chapter in our lives!"

Chapter Two

Wednesday – April 18, 2018

Although the events outlined below actually occurred as outlined in various reports by Google, the plot that follows is truly fictional starting with conversations between two generals.

In 1947, the U.N. approved a plan to partition Palestine into a Jewish and Arab state, and although rejected by the Arabs, Israel was officially declared an independent state in 1948.

After this declaration, five Arab nations: Egypt, Jordon, Iraq, Syria, and Lebanon invaded this region declared to be the independent state of Israel. A cease fire agreement was reached in 1949. As part of the temporary armistice agreement, the West Bank became part of Jordon, and the Gaza Strip went to Egypt.

In 1967, in what started as a surprise attack, Israel defeated Egypt, Jordon, and Syria in six days, not only regaining control of its original independent state, but also that of the Gaza Strip, the Sinai Peninsula, the West Bank, and Syria's Golan Heights. This war became internationally known as the "1967 Six-Day War."

An armistice was established, and the region came under Israel's military control. Almost immediately, the Golan Heights began seeing the area being occupied by Israeli inhabitants.

Syria tried to retake the Golan Heights during the 1973 Middle-East war, but their surprise attack went unrewarded. After another armistice was signed in 1974, the U.N. saw fit to place an observation force along the cease fire line, in essence officially recognizing the occupation of the Golan Heights by Israel. Then in 1981, Israel unilaterally annexed the Golan Heights region; a move that was not recognized by many nations.

A CAFÉ SOMEWHERE NEAR DAMASCUS

3:48 P.M. Sitting down together in a café outside the city of Damascus, two generals are discussing the war in Syria and the Golan Heights in particular.

Syrian General, Husam Ahmadi, leads off by speaking directly to Iranian General Gharib al-Tikriti, "Gharib, we don't have the resources to engage Israel directly, but I would like to see them pay somehow for their occupation of our territory."

"What would you say to letting loose with a few rockets into the Golan Heights, just enough to let them know their occupation of Syrian land is really illegal, at least in Syria's eyes? You would have to expect some form of retaliation, but I have the rockets, if you want to give me the go-ahead."

"We have been hit before, and it would be good to let them know that they can't take our land and not suffer any consequences."

"Okay, how hard do you want to hit them?"

"This could be our one and only chance, so I say hit them really hard, but make sure you miss all U.N. observers. We can at least expect we will receive a U.N. resolution of some sort from this action, but if we end up killing any U.N. observers, the action against Syria will be entirely different."

"I will make sure the rockets land well inside the Israeli settlement. I doubt if they have a shield for the Golan Heights as they have for Tel Aviv. What do say we hit 'em tonight after ten o'clock?"

"I'm all for it!"

Thursday - April 19, 2018

10:25 A.M. Many of the inhabitants in Golan that survived last night's devastating attack are wandering around in shock, some picking up treasured family possessions and others just sitting in a daze, on whatever they can find. Members of the military and the Mossad are on hand, inspecting the debris for clues of what took place. What they discover are the shattered remains of what used to be Iranian rockets.

Aaron Levy of Israel's intelligence, the Mossad, and Colonel Goldman of the Army are discussing what they have found. The Colonel turns to Aaron Levy. "It appears that the rockets used last night are clearly Iranian rockets. Why do you suppose Iran would be firing rockets into the Golan Heights?"

"That is rather strange, but that is clearly what happened. My question right now is what direction we take in retaliation. Although the rockets were obviously fired from Syria, they were fired by Iran. And although neither of us knows the reason behind this action, I believe we have to assume Iran was behind it. As a consequence, right now I see our retaliation being directed toward Iran. Do you agree?"

The Colonel responds, "I do agree, and because our initial count of those slain by this action is extremely high, I recommend extremely hard retaliation. I also know we can expect some form of warning from the U.N. guarding us against any extreme retaliation, but if the tables were turned and the U.N. administration building was hit by an Oklahoma type IED, the outcry would be entirely different."

"What do you have in mind, Colonel?"

"That I will have to discuss with the Prime Minister!"

Friday - April 20, 2018

Prime Minister Ira Kaplan stands and greets Colonel Goldman as he enters the Prime Minister's office. "Can I get you some coffee or tea, Colonel?"

"No, thank you, sir!"

"Well, Colonel, what can you tell me about what happened in Golan?"

"What we discovered will shock you! Amongst all the debris, Aaron Levy was the first to discover the shattered remains of several rockets, and upon close examination, saw enough to positively identify them as belonging to Iran. Neither one of us could figure why Iran would be firing rockets into the Golan Heights, but the facts don't lie. For whatever reason, we have to assume Iran was directly involved and responsible for what happened. Also, we can expect to be highly criticized by the U.N. for any retaliatory action we take, but Mister Prime Minister, the people who settled in Golan suffered extremely high casualties last night. We are still counting the dead. It's my opinion, sir, that we hit Iran hard."

"Well, I'm not anxious to see more people killed. This is what I am going to recommend: 1. Our U.N. Ambassador appear before the General Assembly, displaying pictures of the carnage, calling out the number of people killed and physically harmed. 2. Also display the shattered rockets clearly exhibiting the connection to Iran. 3. Hit Iran where it hurts the most with least amount of human suffering. Bomb their oil fields. Don't take them all out, maybe a third to a half. It will take them some time to get the wells back into action. The Iranian people are not to blame for what happened last night, but the government of Iran is as corrupt and evil as Satan, the devil himself."

Chapter Three

Wednesday - April 25, 2018

10:00 A.M. A special session of the General Assembly has been called, and Israel's U.N. Ambassador steps to the podium and begins to address all those in attendance.

While the Ambassador is displaying pictures of the carnage and shattered remains of the rockets used in the Golan Heights raid, bombers from Israel have taken off and are well on the way to Iran's oil fields.

When the Ambassador had finished his speech, not a sound was heard, no show of acceptance or approval, no words of defiance; just complete silence. Everyone was speechless. There wasn't one person to condemn Iran's action. People were either overwhelmed by what they saw or too sympathetic toward Iran to condemn their actions.

The bombing of Iran's oil fields was carried out precisely as planned, while Israel's Ambassador was giving his speech to the General Assembly. And when it was over, half of Iran's oil wells were completely destroyed, and not a single person was known to be harmed. The fields appeared to be entirely free of any personnel overseeing the operation of the pumps.

News of Israel's raid was quick to follow the Ambassador's speech, and the Assembly, which was as silent as a church at midnight earlier, suddenly burst into the loud ranting and raving of several nations. Knowing in advance of the bombing raid, Israel's Ambassador was quick to leave immediately the moment he finished his speech, being well aware of the uproar and furor that would follow.

Iran's Ambassador was quick to rush to the podium and grab the microphone. "Israel's destruction of Iran's oil fields is an outrage. I demand that Israel make full restitution and formally apologize to Iran and this august body for their actions."

Hearing those remarks, Israel's Ambassador returns to the podium, grabs the microphone from Iran's Ambassador, and begins to loudly respond, "After Iran's despicable and absolute evil, satanic, inhuman slaughter of thousands in the Golan Heights, you have the utter gall to come up here and ask for an apology? I'll see you in hell first! That raid on your oil fields, where loss of life was none to minimal, was extremely small recompense for the thousands of innocent lives you took in Golan. I'll see you in hell!"

With that Israel's Ambassador hands the microphone back and walks out of the room, leaving Iran's Ambassador standing there speechless.

Chapter Four

Tuesday – May 8, 2018

9:36 A.M. Prime Minister Kaplan has made arrangements to see the Turkish Prime Minister about joining the Mid-East Assembly of Nations in their fight against Iran. His plane, known as Israel One, has just lifted off from Ben Gurion Airport and the pilot, Frank Abrams, has contacted departure control to request flight plan instructions to Ankara, Turkey. Little does Frank know that Hezbollah in Lebanon is dialed into Israel's departure control frequency and has heard every word of his request for a flight plan to Ankara. What makes this event so special is that Frank has identified the plane as "Israel One." This immediately tells Hezbollah that Israel's Prime Minister is on that plane that has just taken off on a flight to Ankara. This information is relayed to HQ and Hezbollah goes into spontaneous action, keeping a close watch of this flight by in-flight instructions and radar. When the plane reaches a point some forty miles off the coast of Lebanon, several surface-to-air missiles are launched. One makes a direct hit of the right wing, shattering its aileron, spinning the plane out of control, and forcing it to crash land into a fairly rough sea. The plane hits the water hard with a slightly nose high attitude, staying partially afloat. Then Frank bolts out of his seat to check the condition of everyone on board only to see his co-pilot sitting there in a daze with a severe gash over his right eye. Frank asks, "Levi, are you alright?"

"My head hurts like hell, but I think I'll be okay. Go check on the Prime Minister!"

Frank enters the main cabin to see the Prime Minister up and checking on several members of his cabinet, as well as some aides. A few show various signs of shock.

Frank asks, "Are you alright, Mister Prime Minister?"

"Yes, I'm okay, but a few of my people need attention. How long can we stay afloat and will anyone rescue us?"

"Put on your life vest, Mister Prime Minister, and if you can, help me to put on these life vests on everyone else."

As Frank and the Prime Minister are helping everyone on board with life vests, Levi joins in, as well. Frank then tries to quell the Prime Minister's fears by telling Levi to break out the inflatable life raft. Levi grabs the raft from overhead storage, opens a side door, and throws out the raft while simultaneously pulling a D ring that immediately inflates it.

Opening the side door, however, causes water to come wildly gushing into the cabin, making it extremely difficult to exit the plane. Levi is the first to exit. He swims to the raft, grabs a paddle, and begins paddling back to the side door. By this time, the plane is half under water, and people are struggling to leave the plane. One by one, they dip down below the surface of the water to exit, and Levi is there to help them into the raft. The Prime Minister and Frank, the pilot and captain of the plane, are the last to leave. As everyone on board the raft settles in, each one in his own way is thanking God that he has spared them, then they watch as they see the plane finish sinking slowly out of sight.

The Prime Minister is sitting next to the Captain. "Captain, how long do you think it will take us to be rescued?"

"Our exact location is known by in-flight control, and Ben Gurion has been alerted. Helicopters will be immediately dispatched and should be here in about an hour, maybe less."

Besides Ben Gurion being alerted, Hezbollah also has been tracking the action and has sent several helicopters to the scene from Beirut with armed militia. And because Beirut is much closer to the scene than Tel Aviv, they are the first to arrive.

The first helicopter on the scene calls to his contact at Hezbollah. "We have the Prime Minister in sight. He is sitting in a raft next to a person in uniform, whom I have to assume is the pilot."

"You have to pick up the Prime Minister. You won't be able to do this without a fight from everyone on board the raft. Do what you have to do to get him, even if it means rappelling several armed militia into the raft and disabling anyone that gets in the way. Use your weapons if you have to, but get him!"

Two of the helicopters rappel three armed men each into the raft. Several shots were fired into the air on the way down. Some of the Prime Ministers cabinet members tried as best they could to come to the Prime Minister's defense, but fists are very rarely a good match against guns. The Prime Minister is grabbed and held by two, huge members of the militia, and the rappel line is given two quick yanks, giving the signal to start hauling them back in. The same signal is also given to the second helicopter.

As the helicopters fly out of sight, heading back to Beirut, Israel's helicopter arrives on the scene and begins lowering a line with a harness attached at the end. When the first person hauled up is not the Prime Minister, the first question asked is, "Where's the Prime Minister?"

"The Prime Minister has been abducted by Hezbollah and the Lebanese militia."

"What? I can't believe it! Does Lebanon really want to take on the Israeli Army? This calls for all-out war!"

Chapter Five

Wednesday – May 9, 2018

7:35 A.M. The remaining members of Israel's cabinet have been called into emergency session and elected acting Prime Minister, Abram Kohl, as interim Prime Minister. Then the meeting immediately turns to the Minister of War, Jacob Rosen, in attendance.

"How do we handle this situation, Jacob? What is our first move?"

"Before we start any bombing raids on Lebanon, which will accomplish nothing at this point, we must first contact the Lebanese President to ask him why he has abducted the Prime Minister of Israel and what he plans to do with him. Depending on his answer, we will then decide our next plan of action. Do you concur, Mister Prime Minister?"

"I certainly do concur, and I will leave right now to give him a call. If you wish to continue, I shall return in a few minutes to give you his answer."

Abram Kohl returns to his office and asks his secretary to get Lebanese President, Ibrahim Mustaffa, on the line. Tell the person answering that Israel's interim Prime Minister, Abram Kohl, is on the phone waiting to speak to him about a very urgent matter that suddenly has risen. I'm sure he'll know what I'm talking about."

Three minutes later, President Ibrahim Mustaffa picks up the phone. "Mister Prime Minister, what a surprise! What can I do for you this morning?"

"Just one very important thing: You can return Israel's true Prime Minister back to Israel, immediately! I am the newly elected Interim Prime Minister forced to take this position because the plane carrying Prime Minister Kaplan on a mission to Turkey was shot down this morning by members of your Hezbollah and taken prisoner. I have just one question: How and when will you be returning the Prime Minister back to Israel?"

"This is all news to me. You are the first one to tell me of this unfortunate occurrence. I will have to look into this matter and get back to you."

"You have to realize this is an extremely urgent matter. I need to hear your answer as early as possible and no later than later this morning."

"I'll call you back as soon as I have an answer for you, but no later than this morning."

11:38 A.M. Interim Prime Minister Kohl is sitting in his office, eagerly waiting to hear from the Lebanese President. He begins muttering to himself, *What is taking so long?* Little beads of perspiration have formed on his worried brow, as he begins pacing the floor. *I should have heard from him by now.* The phone rings. He picks it up.

"This is President Mustaffa. I have some rather bad news for you. Hezbollah has turned Prime Minister Kaplan over to the government authorities of Iran late this morning, and I just found out about it."

"I don't know whether to believe you or not. How could you let that happen? If Iran has him now, we may never see him again. Right now, you are saying you no longer have him, and I would venture to say that if I contacted Iran, they would deny having him, too."

Chapter Six

Wednesday – May 9, 2018

6:38 P.M. The plane carrying the Prime Minister from Beirut has just landed at Mehrabad International Airport in Tehran. He is greeted by none other than the President of Iran, himself, Tahir al Majid. The Prime Minister steps off the plane in handcuffs and shackles surrounding his ankles, making it difficult to do anything but take baby steps in trying to walk.

"Well, this is an honor and a pleasure to meet you, Prime Minister Kaplan. It's too bad we have to meet under these circumstances, but because of you, we have lost half of our oil production capacity. What better way to cripple a country, right? And because of what you have done, Mister Prime Minister, what we have planned for you will not be pleasant. A crime of this magnitude calls for severe punishment. The fact that you are the head of the guilty country makes it even worse."

"Right now, my only regret is that I didn't order the entire destruction of your oil fields, instead of only half. I was thinking of how total destruction would affect the welfare of your people. I have no ill feeling toward them, only the government that controls them with an iron fist."

"You have no idea what kind of a hole you are digging for yourself at the moment. Everything you have said, I will testify against you when your case comes to trial."

"I can't wait!"

President al Majid turns to Tehran's Police Chief standing by. "Chief, take this prisoner to Evin Prison's interrogation room for questioning."

"It'll be my pleasure, Mister President!"

With the shackles still in place, Prime Minister Kaplan is pushed along, struggling to take every step to a waiting van and shoved inside.

Chief Interrogator Rajid is there at the special entrance for prisoners when the van arrives. Rajid is about six feet tall and weighs almost two hundred and fifty pounds; slightly obese but muscular. His head is shaved, but he has rugged facial hair that goes with his strong, mean, expressionless face. He's the type of person who takes delight in seeing a person squirm.

"Welcome to your new future home, Mister Prime Minister. But before I introduce you to your new surroundings, I have a few questions I need to ask you."

Thursday – May 10, 2018

9:15 A.M. Interim Prime Minister Abram Kohl is in his office and has just placed a call to Iran's President, Tahir al Majid. "Mister President, this is Interim Prime Minister Kohl calling from Tel Aviv. I have been informed that you are now holding Prime Minister Kaplan in your country. I was given this information by Lebanese President Mustaffa. Is this correct?"

"Good morning, Prime Minister Kohl, I have to say you have been correctly informed; your former Prime Minister is now in our hands. It is he who is responsible for the destruction of half of our oil generating capacity; a crime that we do not take lightly and one for which he must suffer the consequences."

"What are you planning to do?"

"He will have to stand trial and take whatever punishment is awarded."

"And what would that likely be?"

"Either death by hanging or life imprisonment!"

"You must be aware of the all-out cry by millions around the world that will take place because of your actions. I am going to call U.N. President Polansky for an immediate emergency meeting to discuss your plans to try our Prime Minister and possibly hang him. This action is outrageous and unheard of by any civilized nation today. You haven't heard the last of me, President Majid."

"You won't be receiving the world's sympathy that you think you will be receiving!"

"Goodbye, Mister President!"

9:35 A.M. Roman and Rina have just arrived at their office in New York City, and their secretary informs them that they have had several calls from a Mister Aaron Levy, Director of Intelligence in Tel Aviv, who wants you to call him the moment you arrive."

"Thanks, Jacquie! Please get him back on the line for us."

Rina and Roman both get on a phone, but Rina is the first to speak. "Aaron, you made several calls trying to get hold of us. I can imagine what you have on your mind. Roman and I heard the news last night that the Prime Ministers plane to Turkey was shot down. Nothing further was said. Do you have any additional information?"

"Yes, I do! We have found out that he was captured and taken prisoner by Hezbollah's militia. And Lebanese President Mustaffa informed Interim Prime Minister Kohl that Hezbollah in turn handed him over to the Iran authorities. So, as of right now, our Prime Minister is somewhere in Iran and undergoing who knows what? The two of you know Iran better than anyone else I know, outside maybe of Azira. You have worked with agent Azira before. The three of you should make a good team. I realize you both are still wanted dead or alive in Iran, but with your skills, you have managed to outwit them before, and I have confidence you can do it again. I desperately need your help. Can I depend on you?"

Roman and Rina both answer, "Aaron, you know you can!"

"Great, I knew you wouldn't let me down."

Roman asks, "Would you be able to give us a hand getting into the country?'

"Roman, remember how the American Seal Team put you ashore before on the coast of Iran? Well, I will inform the State Department of the situation, and I am sure we will get their cooperation into talking the Navy to help us one more time. The Navy is right in the area. I'll give the State Department a call right now and get back to you."

Roman and Rina both respond, "We will be waiting for your call."

Still Thursday – May 10, 2018, in Tel Aviv

10:46 A.M. Israel's Prime Minister's wife, Teresa Kaplan, has placed a call to Interim Prime Minister Kohl. "Mister Kohl, I have heard the news over the T.V. that my husband's plane to Turkey was shot down in international waters. Do you know what his condition is right now? Is he okay?"

"Mrs. Kaplan, I have to apologize to you for not contacting you, but due to circumstances that required my immediate attention, there just wasn't time."

"What circumstances? I know his plane was shot down. Is there something else you are not telling me? Tell me you have recovered him and he is okay!"

"Mrs. Kaplan, what I have to tell you I had no intention of telling you over the phone, but there is hardly any way of avoiding it now. Are you sitting down?"

"Yes, yes, I am sitting down! Please, what is it?"

"After the Prime Minister's plane crashed into the sea off the coast of Lebanon, Hezbollah's helicopters reached him before we could make contact. They pulled him from the inflatable raft he was in and flew him to Beirut. Hezbollah, in turn, handed him over to Iran. Iran has him in custody at the moment."

"What are you doing to get him released?"

"Mrs. Kaplan, it isn't that simple. I have been in conversation with Iran's President this morning, and he has no intention of releasing him, at least not right away. I think he may want keep him as some form of bargaining ploy." Prime Minister Kohl thinks to himself, *I can't tell her right now that Iran is planning to put her husband on trial with the possibility of hanging, remote as it might be. She doesn't have to know that right now.*

"You mean there isn't anything we can do? I'm only a humble housewife, but when a nation's Prime Minister is captured and held prisoner by a foreign power, I would think the nation involved would do anything to get him back… even going to an all-out war."

"I could threaten Iran with an all-out war, but the moment the first bomb is dropped, they would think it only right to kill him. Somehow we have to do this diplomatically if we want to save his life."

"What are you going to do?"

"Before you called, I had planned to call U.N. President Polansky to set up an emergency meeting to discuss the Prime Minister's capture by Iran with the intention of getting the U.N.'s and the world's disdain of the action Iran has taken. With world opinion working against Iran, it might alter the plans that they have for your husband."

"Please, don't let me hold you up!"

Chapter Seven

Thursday – May 10, 2018

6:48 A.M. Prime Minister Kaplan has spent about the last twenty-four hours in a cell they call the "Hole" in Evin Prison and kept awake by alternatingly being forced to stand for four hours and allowed to sit for an hour to wear him down prior to his interrogation. It tends to make the person being interrogated more cooperative in the eyes of the interrogator. It helps lessen the will to resist. The Hole is aptly named as it is bare of any beds, cots, or chairs; just a bare dirt floor with solid wooden walls all around and bars overhead. A fellow inmate was given the job of keeping the Prime Minister awake with threat that if he failed in his job in any way, he would be forced to serve another five years of his sentence. Guards overhead were on hand to observe the conditions below.

A rope ladder is lowered into the hole, and with his hands still in handcuffs and his legs still held in shackles, the Prime Minister is ordered to climb out of the hole. There is nothing firm or solid about a rope ladder, and every step is a struggle. His fellow inmate is ordered to help him up.

Rajid, the interrogator, is on hand to greet the Prime Minister as he manages to get his feet on solid cement.

"Well, Mister Prime Minister, did you enjoy your first night in Evin Prison?" The Prime Minister fails to answer. He immediately gets a crushing fist to his left jaw, leaving him bleeding quite profusely. I asked you a question, and I expect an answer."

Prime Minister Kaplan tries to wipe the blood off his face with his hand-cuffed hands. "Yes, I enjoyed the night. It was a blast!"

The Prime Minister gets another crushing fist to his mouth. "I didn't like your answer. I think you lied to me! Are you feeling tired?"

"Yes, I am quite tired, and that's no lie."

"Just to show you what a charitable heart I have, I am going to provide a chair for you to use."

The Prime Minister is led into another room and shoved into a wooden chair, where he has his arms strapped to the arms of the chair. Floor lamps with bright lights are brought into the room. The lights are turned on and focused on the Prime Minister's face.

Interrogator Rajid grabs the Prime Minister's head, pulling on his hair toward him, saying, "We have Iran's Intelligence Director here who is going ask you a few questions. Tell us what we want to know, and I'll go easy on you. If you don't, it'll be a different story all together. Alright, Director Ghafur, ask away!"

"I will start with something simple. What is your name?"

"My name is Ira Kaplan!"

"What is your title?"

"I am the Prime Minister of Israel."

"Did you give the order the destroy Iran's oil fields?"

"Yes, I did!"

"Why did you give that order?"

"It was given in retaliation of the slaughter of thousands of Israeli citizens killed in the Golan Heights."

"Iran officially had nothing to do with that event."

"It was proven that Iran rockets were used. Who else but Iran would fire them?"

"Tell me, what kind of action can Iran expect as a result of your capture?"

"I really don't know."

Rajid has removed his heavy leather belt and has it doubled up. Taking his belt, he swats it across the Prime Minister's face. "I don't want to hear 'I don't know' answers!"

"What do you expect your Interim Prime Minister will do to free you?"

"He will probably do what he can diplomatically."

"What kind of a man is Interim Prime Minister Kohl? Is he a forceful man or shy by nature?"

"I know him to be a forceful man and not one to take lightly."

"Now I'm going to ask you a question, and I need your best answer. What are the names of Israel's secret agents operating in Iran, and where are they located?"

"I am not privy to that type of information. Only my Intelligence Director would know the answer to that question."

Rajid responds, "I don't like your answer to that question." Using his dou bled up belt, he gives the Prime Minister another horrendous blow to his head.

Seeing Prime Minister Kaplan bleeding profusely, Intelligence Director Ghafur tells Rajid, "I think he really is telling us the truth. I don't think a Prime Minister would know information like that, but I had to ask the question. Take him back to his cell, Rajid. That's all for now!"

"At the moment, I don't have him in a cell. I've been keeping him in the Hole. Will you be asking any more questions, Director?"

"No, not for now, at least!"

Rajid looks down at the Prime Minister, "Well Mister Prime Minister, you're in luck. You're going back into the Hole, but this time we won't bother to keep you awake. You can crawl up into a little fetal position and go to sleep."

The overhead bars are opened and a rope is lowered into the Hole. Next the handcuffs are removed from the Prime Minister, and he is ordered to use the rope to lower himself into the Hole. The overhead bars are then closed,

Rajid looks down and with a raspy voice yells, "Have a good sleep your lordship!" all the while roaring with laughter as he walks away.

CHAPTER EIGHT

Thursday – May 10, 2018

11:18 A.M. Interim Prime Minister Kohl has just placed a call to U.N. President Polansky.

"Mister President, I am Interim Prime Minister Kohl of Israel. As you must be fully aware by now, Prime Minister Kaplan is in the hands of Iranian authorities, and it is my firm belief that they intend to put him on trial. Knowing how Iranian justice works where a person is guilty until proven innocent, his outcome is almost predetermined. I would like to discuss the possibility of calling an emergency meeting of the General Assembly to put pressure on Iran to release Prime Minister Kaplan. It is unheard of in this day and age of the civilized world to capture a head of State and put him on trial."

"Put together your thoughts on this matter, and I will call an emergency meeting to let you address the Assembly."

"Thank you, Mister President!"

• • • • •

Friday – May 11, 2018

11:30 A.M. The General Assembly has been called into an emergency meeting, and Interim Prime Minister Kohl has assumed his position at the podium.

"I want to thank you all very much for responding so quickly to this emergency meeting request. The emergency is real and very dire. How many in this room can say that at any time in your nation's history you had your Head of State captured by a foreign power and put on trial? I venture to say that not a nation here can honestly say that, yet that is exactly what has happened to the Prime Minister of Israel. On a mission to Turkey, the plane carrying him was shot down by Iranian missiles. While still in the water, nearby Hezbollah helicopters picked him up and flew him to Beirut. From there he was flown to Tehran and met by Iran's President al Majid. I have talked with President al Majid, and he informed me that Prime Minister Kaplan will stand trial and if convicted, will either be hanged or serve life imprisonment; most likely in Iran's infamous Evin Prison."

At this point, Iran's U.N. Ambassador gets up and begins shouting, "He will get what he deserves. He ordered the destruction of half our oil fields. He'll only get what's coming to him."

President Polansky jumps to the podium and begins pounding the gavel. "Order! We must maintain order in this Assembly. Addressing the Ambassador from Iran, he says, "You'll have your chance to speak. Please sit down! Please continue Mister Interim Prime Minister!"

"It is true what the Ambassador from Iran declared. The raid on Iranian oil fields was ordered by Prime Minister Kaplan. It was done in retaliation for the slaughter of several thousand innocent civilians in the Golan Heights who were trying to live normal peace loving lives. In considering what action should be taken, Prime Minister Kaplan did not want to see the loss of human life taken in return. It was his thought that the Iranian people are good people and killing them would be evil. Also, it would only inflame an already bad situation, yet he felt Israel had to answer in some way. What better way than to cut their oil supply. There would be little or no human suffering, but it would cut Iran's income needed for sponsoring terrorist activity and developing weapons of mass destruction. We should note that the Prime Minister didn't order the complete destruction of Iran's oil fields, which he could have done. He felt for the sake of the Iranian people, he couldn't do that.

"So, I implore you for your help and assistance in putting as much pressure as you can on the nation of Iran to free the Prime Minister of Israel. He could have taken retaliatory action of a much stronger nature, but for the sake of the Iranian people, he didn't."

Chapter Nine

Friday – May 11, 2018

9:46 A.M. Roman and Rina are in their office, sitting at their desks discussing the recent abduction of Israel's Prime Minister when the phone rings. Their secretary, Jacquie, picks up the phone. "It's Mister Aaron Levy on the line for you."

"Hello, Roman and Rina! Are you both on the line?"

They both answer, "Yes, Aaron, we're both here!"

"I'm afraid I have some bad news. The U.S. Navy won't be able to help us this time. They are operating in the Persian Gulf, but not necessarily close to Iran at the moment. We will have to talk about another way of getting you into the country. How do you feel about flying to Baku in Azerbaijan and taking a fishing boat to Now Shahr? You are both familiar with a trip of this kind, only this time you would be sailing into Now Shahr, instead of sailing from it. What do you say? What do you think? You could rent a car there and drive to Tehran!"

Roman looks at Rina to get her response. She looks agreeable to the idea and nods her head yes and adds, "I just hope we don't run into any heavy weather on the way!"

Aaron Levy asks, "Do you still both have your Iranian passports?" They both assure Aaron that their passports are up to date.

"Good! How soon can I expect you on the job in Tehran?"

Roman responds, "Well, let's see, today is the eleventh; we'll try to be in Baku by Monday the fourteenth and sailing to Now Shahr, another two to three days. I estimate we should be Tehran on the seventeenth."

"Good, contact Azira when you get there. She'll be expecting you. As I said, the three of you will make a good team. Azira will keep me informed of your progress. Good luck to you both! Words cannot thank you enough for your help!"

Rina responds, "Aaron, you needn't thank us now. Save your thanks until the Prime Minister is safely back in Israel."

Aaron ends by saying, "Then we can all celebrate. Goodbye, and good luck!"

"Goodbye, Aaron!"

Monday – May 14, 2018

2:38 A.M. Roman and Rina landed at Heydar Aliyev International Airport earlier and have just arrived at the port of Baku.

"Rina, we're in luck; we got here at the right time of day. The fishing fleet is still in the harbor. Let's scout around a bit to see if any boats are getting ready for a day of fishing."

Rina cringes a little bit. "I can't say I'm exactly looking forward to this."

After a few minutes, Rina calls Roman's attention by pointing to a particular boat. "Roman, doesn't that boat look a little familiar to you?"

"It sure does! It's the Kutum Quest, Jasim's boat. It's a little odd to see his boat here. Let's go aboard and see if he's up yet. If he intends to do any fishing, he's either up or will be getting up soon."

Still carrying their luggage, they walk aboard the gang plank and drop their luggage on deck with a rather loud thump. That thump brings Jasim on deck from the cabin below. He shouts out, "Well, I can't tell you how oddly surprised I am at this moment to see the two of you here on my boat at this time of the morning. What on earth are you doing here?"

Roman counters with, "I know this sudden appearance is highly irregular, and I can imagine what you must be thinking, but Rina and I need your help. You are already aware of our mission in life as covert agents, and we need your help in getting us back into Iran. You must know by now that the Prime Minister of Israel is now a prisoner of Iran. I'm sure it was on T.V. and in all the papers. What are your feelings about that?"

"It's hard for me to say. I hate to see him captive, as I hate to see anyone a captive of Iran, especially a head of State, but as I understand it, he ordered the destruction of Iran's oil fields. Shouldn't Iran have some right of retribution?"

Roman continues, "This whole mess that we have today started when Iranian rockets were used to shell the civilian inhabitants of the Golan Heights. They were the cruel pawns of someone's hatred. Those rockets killed several thousand people and severely wounded thousands more. What kind of action do you think Israel's Prime Minister should have taken? Just raise his hands and say, 'How awful!' What would you have done, Jasim?"

"I really don't know!"

"Well, the Prime Minister wasn't left the luxury of that type of response. He felt he took the only action open that would take no or very few human lives. What's more, he ordered a partial destruction of Iran's oil fields, not total destruction, which would have been easy for him to do. I am told he was thinking of the Iranian people by ordering a partial destruction. So, now you have the full story! Will you help us, Jasim? We really need transportation to Now Shahr."

"Stow your bags in the cabin, Roman, and you and Rina try to make yourselves as comfortable as possible. We have to begin making the ship ready to get underway."

Roman asks, "How long do you think it will take us to get to Now Shahr, Jasim?"

"Well, as you know from our previous trip, it is exactly two hundred and sixty nautical miles from Baku to Now Shahr. If we sailed directly to Now Shahr, we could probably make it in about two days. But, Roman, I have to remind you, this is primarily a fishing boat, not a cruise liner. We will be spending sometime fishing on the way. It will also depend on how much foul weather we have on the way."

Hearing that, Rina asks Jasim, "Jasim, do you still have that bottle of seasick pills on board?"

Laughing, he says, "Yes, Rina, at the head of the bunk where you found it last time." Jasim looks at the ship's bell momentarily and says, "I have to wake up the crew."

Jasim walks over, and grabbing the clapper of the ship's bell, begins ringing it with enough gusto to wake the dead. Rina begins holding her ears and tells Roman, "I'm heading for my old bunk. Wake me up when we get there!"

This brings on a few contained laughs from Roman and Jasim, as one by one members of the crew begin making their way on deck.

4:00 A.M. Jasim begins giving orders to start hoisting sails and at the same time orders, "Cast off the stern line! Cast off the bow line!"

As the Kutum Quest slowly begins to make its way out of the harbor, Roman, looking for something to do, walks over to Jasim manning the helm and asks, "Jasim, would you care to have someone extra giving the crew a little hand?"

"Are you volunteering?"

"It looks like it's going to be a long trip, and I need to keep busy."

"Have you ever had any experience as a member of a crew aboard a sailing boat before, especially a fishing boat?"

"No, I haven't, but it doesn't look like it would be that hard."

"You may change your mind before this trip is over. Go below in the cabin and find some clothes to wear. You can't do anything in that business suit you're wearing."

"Thanks, Jasim!"

"Never mind that now; save your thanks until we reach Now Shahr. You may be singing a different tune by then."

Roman descends into the cabin below and begins changing into some rather scrubby, well-worn work clothes. Rina can hardly contain herself, asking, "What are you doing?"

"What does it look like I'm doing? I'm going to give the crew a hand, and I very well can't do that wearing a business suit."

At this point, Rina has a hard time picturing Roman working as a member of the crew. It's so out of character for him. She begins to laugh a little. "What has happened to the suave, debonair Roman Hawk I used to know? If your friends in the CIA and the FBI could only see you now."

"Rina, I just can't sit around and do nothing. And right now, you and Jasim are the only ones in the know. If you care to see a working man work, come on up topside."

With that, Roman climbs to the main deck and reports to Jasim at the helm. "Okay, Jasim, give me an order. How can I help out?"

"Report to Samir! He's the huge hulk of a man tying off a line around a cleat on the starboard side."

Roman walks over to him and offers his hand and says, "Samir, my name is Roman Hawk. I have volunteered to work as a member of the crew, and Jasim said I should report to you."

"You don't look like anyone who has ever been a member of a crew, have you?"

"No, I haven't. This will be a new experience for me!"

"Are you in need of work? Is that why you are taking on this job?"

"No, Samir, Jasim offered to take my wife and me to Now Shahr. It's going to be at least a two day trip, and I like to keep busy."

"I haven't talked to Jasim, but I am sure we will be doing some fishing on the way, so if you wish to keep busy, you'll get your wish. We can always use an extra good hand, and you look big and strong enough to help. What did you say your name is?"

"Roman Hawk!"

"Well, Mister Hawk, you can start by giving me a hand repairing some of these nets."

"Samir, it'd be an honor to help you, and you can start by calling me, Roman, not Mister Hawk."

"Okay, Roman, grab one of those nets on the deck there, look for any spots that need repair, and watch me."

• • • • •

7:38 A.M. Samir and Roman have spent the last three hours repairing nets, along with several other members of the crew. During that time, Roman has met and become very good friends with everyone on board, but at the same time, to them, Roman appears to be like a fish out of water. They are all glad to have him working with them, but at the same time they know this is not his kind of work.

Samir calls over to Roman, "Come on, Roman, you've been working almost three hours, and it's time to grab a bite."

The ship's cook has been busy in the galley making breakfast, and one by one, each member of the crew picks up a small tray of food, then finds a small spot on deck to eat.

• • • • •

8:23 A.M. The crew begins throwing the nets overboard and starts trawling. Roman asks Samir, "What kind of fish do you hope to catch, Samir?"

"We are looking for Caspian roach, carp or catfish. Jasim has been sailing the Caspian for over thirty-eight years, and I believe he knows these waters better anyone alive. He tells us where and when to throw out the nets. I believe this particular area is good for catfish. We'll trawl for a while and see what we can come up with."

After a couple of hours, Rina decides she has had enough rest and comes out on deck to a cacophony of loud whistles and wolf calls. Roman yells out, "Okay, guys, you can calm down now. I want you to meet my wife, Rina. She has been resting down below ever since she came on board around three this morning. Rina, walk around and shake hands with these fellas. They really are a good bunch once you get to know 'em."

Rina works her way through out the deck, introducing herself and shaking hands as she moves along. When she has finished, Roman says, "As a word of caution, just because Rina is small, please for your own sake, don't ever try to get fresh with her. She could toss you overboard in an instant, and there would be nothing that you could do about it."

Samir, by far the largest member of the crew, can't contain himself. He walks over to Roman with a look of complete disbelief, "You're going to tell me I have to be cautious of her? What little I have seen of Rina, I like her very much, but to tell me I have to be cautious of her is a little farfetched."

"Maybe you would like a little free home demonstration!"

Rina responds, "Wait a minute, Roman. I'm not dressed for what you have in mind."

Samir responds, "I knew she would try to back out gracefully!"

Feeling she might very well have to defend herself with possibly any member of this crew, Rina retorts, "Please give me five minutes to change."

Five minutes later, Rina appears on deck wearing jeans, sneakers, and a roomy sweatshirt.

Samir, a man of two-hundred and ninety pounds and bulging muscles, looks at Rina and begins to laugh. "Roman, I can't believe I'm doing this. This is so utterly ridiculous. I'm afraid of hurting her!"

Roman counters with, "I felt the same way once. I think it is only fair that I should warn you that Rina has a black belt masters in Tae Kwon Do, Karate, and Jiu Jitsu and has taught martial arts for a number of years."

Samir, in turn, counters with, "I don't care how many black belts she has; there is no way she can come out on top in this thing."

"Okay, Samir, don't say I didn't warn you! You and Rina take positions in this open area of the deck, about two meters apart. I'll clap my hands; then Samir, do your best."

Rina and Samir take their positions on deck as the crew forms a circle around them. "Are you both ready?" Rina and Samir nod their heads yes. A second later, Roman claps his hands, and Samir rushes head on toward Rina. Rina is expecting this, and as he starts to grab her, Rina performs a little Jiu Jitsu by using his weight and strength against him and flips Samir to the deck. Getting up, Samir can't believe what happened. Not to be out done, Samir again rushes toward Rina, who has made her way to the gunwale. As he is about to grab her, she again uses his weight against him and flips Samir overboard into the cold Caspian Sea.

Throwing a life preserver to Samir, Roman shouts, "Man overboard!" This is followed by the crew throwing Samir a line and hauling him on board. The crew at the same time is doing everything they can to prevent from laughing as they know Samir well enough that he could and would make it rough on them.

Dripping wet, Samir walks over to Rina to shake her hand. "I come in peace. I just want to shake your hand, lady. You are one person that I can truly say got the better of me. I'll never underestimate you again, and if any one of my crew does anything to offend you, you just let me know. He won't do it again!"

"Samir, please call me, Rina!"

"Alright, Rina!" And they shake hands.

Chapter Ten

Wednesday – May 16, 2018

6:23 P.M. Evening is just beginning to settle in when the Kutum Quest pulls up alongside the dock in Now Shahr.

Jasim extends his hand to Roman, and Rina adds, "I hope I got you here in time for your next caper, Roman. You two make a great couple."

"The timing is perfect, Jasim. I hope we meet again soon!"

Rina responds, "I second that motion!"

Samir, who is also standing by, walks over to Rina and asks, "May I kiss your hand, Rina?"

"Of course, you may, Samir!"

This huge hulk of a man bends down low and grasps Rina's hand, as her hand almost disappears within his. He gently kisses the back of Rina's hand and then whispers to himself, "What a delicate flower! It's hard to believe that anyone so lovely could be so deadly at the same time." Then, rising up, Samir adds, "It was a pleasure meeting you, Rina. The world is a better place because of you!"

Rina responds, "I have to say, the feeling is mutual!"

At that moment, a police car pulls up on the dock. Fortunately, Roman and Rina are hidden by the raised portion of the cabin.

Roman tells Jasim, "I'm not positive, Jasim, but I think the police here may still know me. I've got to avoid them somehow."

Jasim grabs Roman and pulls him over further out of sight. "You are already wearing crew member clothes. Keep them on and I'll dirty your face a little with some dirt off the deck here and a little grease. Here, wear this cap to cover your hair."

Then Roman asks, "What about Rina? They will certainly want to know what a woman is doing aboard a fishing boat."

Samir, who is still standing by, says, "Don't worry about her! I'll carry her ashore in my large duffle bag."

Roman asks, "Can you actually do that, Samir?"

"Absolutely, no problem!" Samir descends into the cabin, comes back with his oversized duffle bag, and tells Rina, "Hop in! I'll try to be as gentle as I can."

Rina responds, "I know you will, Samir." Rina steps into the oversized bag and crouches down as Samir draws a strong line at the top closed.

With Roman and Rina about as secured as Jasim and Samir can get them, Jasim, Samir with his duffle bag over his shoulder, and Roman walk down the gang plank in full view of the police.

One officer approaches Jasim and questions him, "How was the fishing, Jasim?"

"Officer al Sadi, what a pleasure! It was a good trip. I had a good haul!"

"I know you ordinarily carry a seven-man crew. I see you've picked up an extra man."

"Yes, he came to me before we left and said he needed the work, so I left port with eight men. He turned out to be a good man, and we needed him with the haul we brought in."

"I thought I knew everybody in this town. I think I'd like to meet him."

Jasim calls over to Roman, who is now posing as Ibrahim al Majid. "Ibrahim, this police officer was just mentioning that he thought he knew everyone in town but didn't recognize you and would like to meet you."

Roman walks over and addresses the officer, "You wanted to see me, sir?"

"Yes! I was just telling Jasim that I thought I knew everyone in town, but you are a stranger to me. And people I don't recognize in this small town I always ask to see some identification. Could I please see some identification?"

Roman pulls out his fake driver's license identifying him as Ibrahim al Majid.

The officer responds, "Ibrahim al Majid! Your license says you come from the town of Tabas. What are you doing in Now Shahr, Ibrahim?"

"Work was a little slow in Tabas, and I heard that fishing from Now Shahr was quite good right now, so I thought I might find work here."

"What kind of work do you normally do in Tabas?"

"I work as a plumber."

"Your face looks vaguely familiar! Have we ever met before?"

"I am sure we haven't; that is, unless sometime in the past you visited the town of Tabas."

"I guess you must be right. I'm sorry I troubled you."

"That's quite alright, officer!"

After Officer al Sadi drives off, Roman and Samir still carrying Rina over his shoulder in his duffle bag, get into Jasim's car, and drive off a few blocks out of Officer al Sadi's sight. Rina, who up to this time has been weirdly silent, starts screaming, "Will somebody please let me out of this sack? I'm not sure I'll ever be the same."

Getting out of the car, Samir lowers the bag from his shoulder and gently places it on the ground. "Hold on, Rina. I'll have you out in just a second."

"Wow! I can't tell you how great it feels to be free to move my legs and arms. At the same time, I have to thank you, Samir, for a great job getting me off the boat. Now that it's over, I have to laugh. The whole thing was pretty funny."

Roman looks around the area and says, "Jasim, I'm not really familiar with this part of town. Is there a place nearby to rent a car?"

"Actually, we are pretty close to the business district. I think it's safe to drive you there now."

"Thanks, Jasim! Before we go, Rina and I need to say goodbye to Samir, who has been a real big help."

They both walk up to Samir, still standing by off to the side, and offer their hands in parting. Rina is the first to offer her hand. "Samir, it has been a real pleasure knowing you. You are one person I'll never forget."

"And, Rina, I can truthfully say, you are one person I'll never forget, as well." Then, saying with a laugh, "Anyone that's good enough to toss me overboard, I gotta remember. You truly are one special person!"

Roman adds, "I second everything Rina mentioned. We both think a lot of you." Shaking his hand, he says, "Till we meet again!"

Jasim drops Roman and Rina off in front of the auto reservations. Roman and Rina reach through the driver's window and shake Jasim's hand goodbye. Roman says, "Goodbye, Jasim! I have the strangest feeling that this is not the last time you and I will be seeing each other!"

"I think you are probably right, Roman. I hope you both are successful in whatever you have planned." Jasim waves as he drives off.

Roman and Rina spend a few minutes renting a Fiat, then head for Tehran.

"Rina, it's eight-fifteen. We should be in Tehran by eleven-thirty."

Meanwhile, Officer al Sadi has returned to the station, still wondering when and where he remembers seeing Roman's face before. He sits down with Police Chief al Karim. "Chief, I was just down at the town's boat dock when Jasim Muzahim's boat arrived. I know he normally carries a seven-man crew, but this time I noticed he had eight men. I questioned the eighth man. His driver's license said he was from Tabas, but somehow his face looked slightly familiar, like I had seen him some place before, but where? Let me glance through our records. Maybe I can come up with something.

Officer al Sadi spends forty-four minutes scanning through records dating back eight years when he suddenly discovers Roman's mug shot. "Chief, I've got it! I've found him in these records dating back to the year twenty-ten. The man I saw today is Roman Hawk, but he had a fake driver's license with the name Ibrahim al Majid. The big question now is: What is he doing back in Iran eight years later? I think we need to alert Chief Abbas in Tehran that Roman Hawk could be making his way there."

"I agree!"

Chapter Eleven

Wednesday – May 16, 2018

11:42 P.M. Minister of War, Jacob Rosen, knocks on the office door of Interim Prime Minister Abram Kohl.

"Please, come in, Jacob! May I get you some coffee or tea?"

"No, thank you, Mister Prime Minister!"

"Please, Jacob, please call me Abram. We have been friends too long to rely on formalities."

"Very well, Abram! What did you want to talk about?"

"As you know, I have discussed the abduction of Prime Minister Kaplan with U.N. President Polansky and addressed the General Assembly. Frankly, in my opinion, talking to that group is like talking to a group of elderly ladies. You may or may not get sympathy for your cause, but don't expect any more than that. I need your thoughts. What kind of action can we take? We can't just sit here and do nothing. We have to do something to get him back. Do you have any thoughts on what we can do?"

"Any military action we would take would definitely get him killed. Any action that we take would have to be, as they say, 'sub-rosa.'"

"Then I think we should get Mossad Director, Aaron Levy, to join us. I'll see if he is free."

Abram Kohl gets Aaron Levy on the line. "Good morning, Aaron, Abram Kohl here. I have Jacob Rosen with me here in my office. We were discussing what action we could take to have Prime Minister Kaplan returned to us. We both agree that military action would only result in having him killed. Jacob and I agree that some sort of secret action will have to be taken. You were first on our list, Aaron. Do you know of any way we could secretly remove the Prime Minister out of Iran?"

"I know of two people working in conjunction with one of our agents already in Iran who have the best chance of enabling his escape. I have already called them, and they should be somewhere in Iran right now."

"Good work, Aaron! What do you know about the people you contacted? Are they the best that you know of?"

"They are the very best! I have had them work for me on multiple occasions, and they have never let me down. They know the city of Tehran and the Iranians better than anyone I know. If anyone can help the Prime Minister escape, they can."

"Let's hope and pray they are successful!"

THE NEXT DAY

12:08 A.M. After driving the last few hours from Now Shahr, Roman and Rina are checking into the Barzan Hotel in Tehran under the names of Ibrahim and Latifa al Majid. Little does either of the know that during the time they were driving, the police station at Now Shahr faxed Roman's mug shot, taken eight years ago, to police headquarters in Tehran. Roman's mug shot was, in turn, wired to all hotels in Iran with instructions to look for this man and notify the police.

As Roman and Rina are signing the register, the hotel clerk on duty was looking at the mug shot of Roman discretely hidden from Roman's view. After signing in, Roman and Rina check into their room and begin getting ready to climb into bed. At the same time, the hotel clerk calls police headquarters.

"Hello, is this the police station?"

"Yes, it is! Who's calling?

"This is the hotel clerk at the Barzan Hotel. I just received this mug shot over the wire a few minutes ago with instructions to notify the police if I saw the man in the photo. He just checked in a couple of minutes ago. He's in room 216."

"Thank you for the call. We will be right over. Don't alert him that we are coming for him!"

"No, I won't!"

Twenty minutes later, the police are knocking on Roman's door. Roman asks Rina, "Who could that possibly be? Who knows we are here but the hotel clerk?"

Roman gets out of bed and on the way to the door, yells, "Who is there?"

"This is the police. Open the door!"

Rina jumps out of bed with the intent of overpowering the police, but then thought if she did, the police would be after her, too, then they would both be on the run. She had to make a split second decision that at least she had to be free to move. *Whatever he does, he will have to do it on his own!*

Roman sees that Rina is not making a move and weighs in his mind, *I could easily overpower the police on the other side of that door, but then I would be on the run and what good could I be then? Better to give myself up and stand trial. Undoubtedly, I will end up in Evin Prison. Actually, I could probably do more to help the Prime Minister escape while a prisoner inside Evin Prison than on the outside. That's what I'll do, I'll go peacefully!*

The police on the other side shout, "Open up this door, or we will come in shooting!"

Roman shouts back, "Please, don't shoot! I'm coming!" Standing there in his pajamas, Roman opens the door and puts his hands up.

"Roman Hawk, get dressed! As an escaped convict, you are under arrest and coming with us."

As soon as Roman is dressed, he is ordered, "Put your hands behind your back," and he is immediately handcuffed. Both knowing that something like this was a possibility, without saying a word, they look at one another, wondering what the future holds, as Roman is hauled out of the room.

Chapter Twelve

Thursday – May 17, 2918

1:36 A.M. Roman has his handcuffs removed and is roughly shoved inside the holding cell he knows so well from his time here eight years ago. He looks around at the filthy characters he is being forced to share his life with and begins to wonder about his immediate future. *Right now, I'm in one hell of a spot. The Prime Minister doesn't know it at this time, but he is depending on me and Rina to help him escape from Evin Prison. I only hope I'm doing the right thing right now and right now the prospects are looking rather grim. Guess I better pick out a spot on this cement floor and try to get some sleep, if I can.*

• • • • •

6:00 A.M. Roman wakes up to hear the familiar rattle of the guard's baton on the cell bars. "All right, you bums, time to get up. C'mon, on your feet!"

Roman gets up and looks around. *The cell is the same, but it appears we have a new class of low life degenerates. Hey, wait a minute!* Looking over into one corner of the cell, Roman sees a familiar face. *I can't believe it! It looks like my friend, Hajid, from eight years ago. What the heck is he still doing here?*

Roman walks over to the corner and sees Hajid still sitting there in a kind of trance, staring into space. *I have to say, he hasn't changed a whole lot. Aside from the clothes he is wearing, they must have given him something to wash and take care of himself, but why would they keep him here?*

Roman bends down to get his attention, looking into his face. "Hajid, it's me, Roman Hawk!"

With his blank stare, Hajid looks up. "Roman Hawk? Do I know you?"

"Yes, you do! You and I spent a short time together in this cell eight years ago. You were being molested by some huge ape, and I came to your rescue. Remember?"

Hajid climbs up off the floor. "Yes, it's coming back to me now. I remember someone big and tall helping me at the time, and then he managed to escape somehow. Was that you?"

"Yes, it was, Hajid! You are beginning to remember, and in case you have forgotten, my name is Roman Hawk."

"I am glad you reminded me. I forgot your name."

"What are you doing here, Hajid? There is no way you were in this cell for eight years."

"I was arrested two weeks ago as part of a protest march. Because I have a familiar face, they picked me out of the crowd, so here I am again!"

"What have you been doing the past eight years, Hajid?"

"I served seven years in Evin Prison, and I've been free about a year. Maybe it's a good thing! I had a hard time making it on the outside. At least I get free food in Evin Prison."

"Well, Hajid, all I can say is, 'Whatever makes you happy!' and it's good to see a friendly face, even under these conditions."

Roman walks over to the cell bars, surveys the surroundings, and thinks to himself, *Well, nothing much has changed here in eight years. They still have the same old guard desk with a lamp on it. The guards have changed, but nothing else has. I wish Hasan were still here. It was good to have a cousin in the police force working right here. I couldn't have made it out of here without him, and he died such a horrible death. Stepping on a land mine! What are the odds of that happening? All those mines planted at the Iran and Iraq border were never completely cleared. Rina was lucky she didn't accidentally step on one.*

· · · · ·

9:45 A.M. Two armed guards approach Roman's cell and shout out, "Roman Hawk, put your hands behind your head and step up to the cell door." The door is opened, Roman is dragged out, and the door is immediately slammed shut. Then, one at a time, they take Roman's left wrist, cuffing it, and then his right wrist, cuffing it behind him.

"Mister Hawk, you have a date with the judge. This way, if you please!"

"Yes, I know the routine."

· · · · ·

10:00 A.M. Roman is led into the same large room as before, eight years ago. Nothing has changed; the judge is sitting behind his elevated bench in civilian clothes. Roman stands on a small platform with his hands in handcuffs behind him. An armed guard stands on either side of him. As Roman waits for the judge to call the court to order, he begins thinking, *Here I am again. I wonder what kind of a sentence I'll get this time. I ended up with five years in Evin Prison before which, thanks to my cousin, Hasan, I never had the pleasure of serving. I won't be so lucky this time. I wonder if I will have the same judge. I hope not!*

The judge announces, "The court will come to order!" Then with a rather wry smile on his face, he addresses Roman, "Mister Hawk, I can't tell you what a pleasure it is to see you again! It has been a long time. If you had not left our fair city voluntarily, you would have served your first sentence of five years in Evin Prison by this time. Unfortunately for you, your escape, and the problems it caused for our judicial system, is going to cost you an additional ten years behind bars at hard labor. You now have to serve a sentence of fifteen years at hard labor. Your sentence will be served at Harbush Prison near the city of Bushehr. Next case!"

Roman is led back to his holding cell, awaiting further transfer to Harbush Prison. On the way, his thoughts are running wild. *This ruins everything!*

I can't be sent to Harbush prison. The sole purpose of giving myself up was to be in the same prison as the Prime Minister so I would at least have some chance of helping him escape. There is absolutely nothing I can do in another prison, not to mention I'll be stuck in that prison for fifteen years. This couldn't be working out any worse than it is.

• • • • •

1:35 P.M. Rina has just signed into the jail cell logbook as Latifa al Majid and runs over to the cell where Roman is standing and tries to kiss him. The cell guard runs over pulls Rina away. "You're not allowed to touch the prisoner. Stand forty centimeters away!"

Rina blows Roman a kiss as she calls out to him, "Roman I can't stand to see you back in this jail cell. This is terrible! What are we going to do?"

"You don't know the worst of it. I have just been given a sentence of fifteen years; not in Evin Prison where I thought I would be sent, but in a place called Harbush Prison near the city of Bushehr on the Persian Gulf. There is no way I can do anything under those conditions. Somehow you will have to make it on your own."

"You know I can do nothing without you, Roman. Much as I hate to, I will have to call Aaron and give him this horrible news. Maybe he will have some ideas."

"Check with Az first; maybe she can come up with some idea of what to do."

"Don't give up hope, Roman. I will be back tomorrow."

"I hope I'm still here tomorrow!"

Rina blows Roman another kiss and waves goodbye.

Chapter Thirteen

Thursday – May 17, 2018

3:25 P.M. Rina has placed a call to Azira at her furniture warehouse. "Hi Azira, it's me, Rina calling. Roman and I just got into Tehran late last night. Don't ask me how or why, but Roman was arrested by the police shortly after we checked into the Barzan hotel. They wasted no time. He had a trial this morning and was given a sentence of fifteen years to be carried out at a place called Harbush Prison, near the city of Bushehr on the coast."

"Oh, I have heard of that place. It has a reputation of being run like a combination old style Southern U.S. chain gang prison and France's Devil's Island. The conditions are strictly inhuman!"

"I wish you hadn't told me that, Azira. Now, I'm not so much worried about the original objective that Roman and I had. We have to help Roman some way."

"Right off hand, I don't see any way we can help him, Rina! I'll discuss the situation with Aaron. Maybe he can come up with some ideas of what we can do. I'll call you back in a few minutes."

"Please, Azira, please give me some reason to hope!"

"I'll call you back in just a few minutes."

Azira places a call to her contact in Jordon who, in turn, scrambles her outgoing conversation by scrambling each word received and instantly sending it on so it sounds garbled to anyone who could be trying to listen in. Mossad

Director, Aaron Levy, has the ability to unscramble the conversation instantly with no hesitations.

"Big A, this is Little A. One half of your duo arrested and being sent to Harbush. Need aid."

"Little A, stand by! Will study and get back."

When Aaron hangs up with Azira, he places a call to CIA Director Fred Graves.

"Hello, Director Graves, Aaron Levy here! Be advised I am speaking on a secure line. I am calling to bring you up to date with the present situation involving Prime Minister Kaplan and the action I have taken to somehow obtain his release from Evin Prison in Tehran. It was generally agreed that military action of any kind, such as bombing Iran again, would only give them cause to kill the Prime Minister. It was also agreed that we would have to use some method of secretly ushering him out of the country. I chose upon the two most qualified people I know that have worked miracles for me in the past, Roman Hawk and Rina Kohl. I knew they would be taking a chance working inside Iran, because of their past experiences in Iran they were both wanted by Iranian authorities. They still agreed to do what they could to obtain the release of the Prime Minister from Evin Prison. I just received devastating news from one our agents in Tehran. Roman was arrested and told to serve his sentence in Harbush Prison near Bushehr on the Persian Gulf. Do you have any recommendations of what action we might take at this time?"

"My line is secure, as well. Thank you for calling and bringing me up to speed, Aaron. As I see it, our first action should be doing all we can to get Roman's release from Harbush Prison, even if it means no more than a transfer to Evin Prison. From what I know about Harbush Prison, escape is next to impossible. I have an agent working Tehran. His name is Sulayman Azzawi. I will contact him, bring him up to date, and ask him to help out in anyway feasible."

"Have him contact our agent in Tehran, Azira Mahdi, who as a cover-up, is manager of Tehran Moving and Storage Company in Tehran. Working together, perhaps they can come up with something, along with Rina Kohl, who is still walking free."

"I'll do that, and I'll have him keep me informed of any progress that is made."

"I'll do the same. Azira Mahdi is quite good at keeping me up to speed."

"Call me again any time, Aaron. It's always good to hear from you."

"And you as well, Fred! Goodbye!"

After hanging up with Fred Graves, Aaron calls Azira on the scrambled line. "I called America. Someone will contact you personally to give you aid in near future. Out!"

Azira now calls Rina. "Where can I meet you?"

"I'm staying at the Barzan Hotel."

"I'll meet you in the lobby in thirty minutes."

. . . . .

5:16 P.M. Azira finds Rina sitting in the Barzan lobby. "Sorry I'm late, Rina. I got held up at the warehouse on an urgent matter. I got hold of Aaron Levy and explained the situation with Roman. He in turn said he called America, undoubtedly, Fred Graves of the CIA, saying someone would be contacting me in the near future to help us in some manner. We will have to wait and see."

"I welcome any help we can get, but unless this someone possesses some hidden mystical power, I can't see right off hand how anyone will be able to get Roman free."

"Don't give up hope, Rina. With the right people working on the outside for Roman, anything is possible!"

"Thanks for your hopeful words, Azira. I'm going back to see Roman and try to give him reason to hope. I'll check with you tomorrow."

"Give Roman my best!"

"I will, Azira!"

. . . . .

7:48 P.M. Rina signs into the cell book log and asks to see Roman Hawk. "Ma'am, he's no longer here. Guards from Harbush Prison picked him up just a few minutes ago. You just missed him."

Rina begins to sob a little and say to herself in a voice barely audible, "Oh, no! I can't believe it. Oh, Roman! Oh, Roman! What am I to do without you? They will treat you like a caged animal in that prison!" Rina finds the nearest chair and sits down crying her heart out. The cell guard pulls out a clean handkerchief and offers it to Rina. "Here, ma'am, it's clean!"

Rina sits in that chair for nearly twenty minutes trying to regain some composure. She wipes the tears from her eyes and returns the guards handkerchief. "Thank you so much! You have been very kind."

"Anything I could do to help, ma'am!"

Rina returns to the Barzan Hotel and calls Azira to let her know that Roman had been picked up by guards from Harbush Prison before she had a chance to see Roman.

"Please, don't worry, Rina. We will get him back some way; I just know we will."

Chapter Fourteen

Friday – May 18, 2018

9:18 A.M. Azira is in her office at Moving and Storage warehouse when her secretary enters her office to say, "There is a gentleman here to see you. His name is Sukayman Azzawi!"

"Thank you, Lamda! Please show him in!"

"Sully, it's so good to see you. It was back in late spring of 2015 when we last worked together."

"Are you still working for Savama as your cover in Iran?"

"Yes, I have a new boss now since the departure of Mahmud Abuzar. I believe I heard that Rina captured him and took him to the United States to be used as a bargaining chip to get her parents released from Evin Prison."

"That is my understanding, too. You'll be seeing her sometime in the near future. You can ask her about it then."

"I had a call from CIA Director Graves asking me to do what I can to help you and Rina Kohl obtain the release of Roman from Harbush Prison. To be honest, Azira, that is a pretty tough nut to crack. But as my dad used to say, if there is a will, there is a way. I will have to study and survey Harbush Prison to find a weakness. Nothing is ever a hundred percent. I'll find a way, even if it means only getting him transferred to Evin Prison. At least it would be getting him out of that hell hole and into the same prison that is holding the Prime Minister."

"I don't know what you can do, Sully, but please contact me any time. I want to do anything I can to help you."

"I'll be sure to do that, Azira. As I said, my first move is to get to Harbush Prison." Sully chuckles a little bit, and then adds, "Primarily, on the outside! I'll try to keep you in touch."

Sully waves goodbye and Azira returns the wave with "Good luck, Sully!"

Friday – May 18, 2018

3:26 A.M. Roman and his guards arrive at Harbush Prison. Roman is still in handcuffs and ankle shackles. The Commandant of Harbush Prison, Izzat Zimam, is standing in front of his office building ready to greet Roman as he steps out of the van carrying him. Izzat carries a cane and walks with a limp as a result of an injury he suffered during the Iran-Iraq war. He very often uses that cane to give a blow to the head or body of any prisoner he sees fit to. Still shackled and handcuffed, he gives Roman a whack across the face with the cane, adding, "That's just a small token of what you can expect when you get out of line. The rules of this prison are posted on the front of this building. Obey them to the letter. Break them, and I'll break you." Addressing the guards holding Roman, he says, "Show him to his quarters!"

Roman is taken to a nearby wooden building holding forty, low-lying wooden bunks using netting and straw to lie on. Only thirty-eight bunks were occupied prior to Roman's arrival. Roman's handcuffs are removed, leaving his ankle shackles in place. The guards leave the building, but not before admonishing Roman, "Talking is not allowed in this room at any time and roll call is at six in the morning. Stand in line outside the building at that time, and don't be late!"

Roman plops himself on top of the straw, muttering to himself, "And I have fifteen years of this? I don't see anyone lasting any more than one or maybe two years under these conditions. I'll just have to take it one day at a time!"

Friday – May 18, 2018

6:00 A.M. Gharib Taha, a prisoner turn-coat given guard duty and better known as a lackey guard, enters the prison's bunk house, begins ringing a loud bell, yelling, "Roll call! Roll call! You have one minute!"

Roman runs out of the bunk house and finds a spot in the line, then one of the guards begins shouting names, followed by a loud "Here!" after each name. Roman is the last one called. Immediately, the same line forms up for breakfast. Each man is given a bowl and a spoon, then some form of liquid concoction is ladled into it.

Roman looks for a place to sit in the eating room then spots someone totally foreign in the group and sits down next to him.

"You look like you could be an American. My name is Roman Hawk, what's yours?"

"John Rivers! You talk like an American, but you look like one of the group. Are you an American?"

"I am a natural born American. My parents emigrated from Iran."

"How did you end up in this place?"

"I think I angered the judge with my comments at my trial. What line of work were you in, John?"

"I am a reporter for the *New York Globe*. I was covering a story that took me to the Turkish and Iranian border, and at some point, I must have crossed over into Iran. I was immediately picked up, tried as a spy, and here I am."

"How long have you been here?"

"I've lost track of time, but I would say six or seven months. You haven't had time to check this place out yet. There is no way of escaping. The walls are made of cement block, about twenty feet high, and topped with high voltage concertina wire. Oh, that's the bell! Breakfast is over. Stick close to me; I'll try to keep you from fouling up. No talking from here on!"

The prisoners line up again and, one at a time, grab an axe from one of the guards while twenty other guards have their rifles out and pointed at everyone in the line. As they enter the two buses on hand, they all observe punishment being administered to a fellow inmate in the center of the compound. He has his arms up and tied to two, large posts with a sign overhead, saying, "Five Lashes for Talking." The buses pull away as they see him being whipped.

After about a twenty-five minute trip, the buses arrive at a wooded area where a portion of the trees have been cut down. It is here where the prisoners are ordered out of the buses and begin chopping down trees with their axes. The prison has been ordered by the government to prepare a way through this wooded area for a road.

• • • • •

7:37 A.M. Roman and the others receive orders of what trees to cut that day, so with their axes, they start wielding away. This particular wooded area is quite old, and the trees are quite large, taking two men the better part of a day to chop down most any tree. Roman and John end up working on the same tree and not saying a word.

As no one is allowed to talk, except for the guards, the day passes by extremely slowly. John and Roman are drowning in sweat, when one of the guards gives the order to stop chopping and begin loading into the buses.

On returning to Harhush, the massive, wooden gate doors open up allowing the buses to enter. The prisoners unload one at a time, handing back the axes they used that day. Then they are ordered to line up against the cement brick wall behind them. Roman begins wondering, *What are they going to do now—have us line up against this cement brick wall and shoot us?*

Once they are all lined up, they are ordered to raise their arms. Roman is thinking, *They are not going to shoot us, even though it sure appears that way. Shooting us would be senseless! Who then would cut the trees for the road they intend to build?*

Roman sees a truck rolled out before them. A gate is dropped from the back end, and a hose is pulled out. Water is turned on, and everyone is hosed down. This lasts three or four minutes. Then, soaking wet, they form another line for a meal that is called dinner consisting of half-baked fish and rice. John and Roman find a spot at a table and sit down together.

John begins the conversation by saying, "This is the only time we are allowed to talk, so whatever you have in mind to say, this is the time to say it."

"Is what we did today the normal routine?"

"Yes, seven days a week, except for Fridays. Prisoners are given one half-hour for prayer. That's why everyone quit work around noon today for half an hour. Oh, and that hosing we just had—that is our once a week bath. After one day, everybody smells pretty bad, but you get used to it. In a word, the living conditions here are inhuman! Every once in a while, someone will make an attempt to escape with the hope of being shot and killed, out of desperation. That is a tough choice to make because if you are not killed as a result of being shot, the punishment you don't even want to think about. Izzat Zimam has a way of wishing you had never been born, as if you don't already feel that way. And don't ever let him hear you say it, but Izzat Zimam is known under everybody's breath as 'Dizzy Izzy.' You couldn't take the punishment."

"Do you know if the editor of your paper has taken any steps to try and obtain your release?"

"Yes, I am sure he is working on it, but I have no way of knowing absolutely. How about you? Do you have anyone trying to obtain your release?"

"I am positive I have people working on it. Their success is hard to say."

Before either one has a chance to say another word, lackey guard Gharib Taha begins ringing the bell, ordering everyone out of the dining hall and into the bunk house.

Roman and John wave to each other, then Roman plops down on his bed of straw and drops off asleep in a matter of a minute.

Chapter Fifteen

Saturday – May 19, 2018

11:21 A.M. Sully pulls into the city of Bushehr. Parking his car, he walks into the nearest café and orders lunch. Sully sits at the counter and strikes up a conversation with the owner.

"Are you the owner of this fine establishment?"

"Yes, I am! You must be new in town, are you?"

"I just arrived a few minutes ago. I'm trying to meet up with a friend."

"What's his name? I may know him. I know just about everyone who is anyone in this small city."

"He just arrived very recently and certainly is not a person of influence. I would be surprised if you knew him. You sound like you know many influential people."

"Yes, I guess maybe I do!"

Sully stops a moment to think. *Dare I ask him about the head of Harbush Prison at this stage of our conversation? Maybe I should get to know this guy better.* My name is Sulayman Azzawi. Most people call me Sully. What is your name, sir?"

He offers to shake hands and says, "My name is Salim Tilfah. It's good to know you, Sully!"

"And I have to say, it is also good to know you, Salim. I have to believe you have lived in Bushehr a long time."

"All my life; that is why I know most everyone around here."

Sully signals to Salim to move to the end of the counter, so that the one person sitting at the other end would not hear them.

"Would you happen to know the person who runs Harbush Prison?"

"Everybody knows that man. He's a monster. I've had him sit down in my diner, and I had to serve him out of necessity."

"What do you know about him?"

"I know him to be some kind of low life who would probably steal the gold from your back teeth, given half a chance. Why are you so interested in Izzat Zimam?"

"Salim, we have known each other for only a very brief time, but I feel I know you to be an honest man of integrity; a person I can trust. Do you mind If I tell you something in confidence?"

"Well, I don't know. I don't know what you want to tell me."

"Based on what you have been telling me about Izzat Zimam, is that his name?"

"If you are referring to the monster in charge of Harbush Prison, yes, that is his name."

"When I first sat down at the counter, I mentioned that I was looking for a friend. What I didn't mention at the time was that my friend is being held in Harbush Prison on a charge normally considered a misdemeanor. I am here in town to see whatever I can do to obtain his release somehow."

"If you are thinking of some form of escape, you can forget it. As I said, I have lived here all my life and know everything that takes place. And I can tell right off, no one has ever escaped from that place and lived to tell about it."

"I had no thought of planning an escape. My only thought was to get him transferred out of there, perhaps back to Evin Prison in Tehran. I know Evin Prison is no picnic, either, but it is a hundred percent better than Harbush. With his low life reputation, would you happen to know of any information you feel you could share with me in the way of illegal activity that he has perhaps is guilty of, but never suffered the consequences?"

"No, I don't, Sully, but I know a few influential people in town who dislike him as much as I do. What's your friend's name?"

"His name is Roman Hawk!"

"Let me scout around a little bit and get back to you. Where are you staying?"

"There is a small Hilton Hotel in town I hear, you can reach me there."

• • • • •

19:16 P.M. Salim picks up the phone and calls someone he knows could very well be a great help: Tahir Maruf, President of the Bushehr National Bank.

"Tahir, this is Salim. I have something I would like to discuss with you when you have a few minutes."

"Salim, my friend, with you I will make the time. I'm not especially busy right now. I'll be right over."

Fifteen minutes later, Tahir Maruf walks into Salim's diner, sits down at the counter, and says, "How about a cup of your fine coffee, Salim?"

"Coming right up!"

Tahir takes a sip then says, "What did you want to talk about, Salim?"

"Let's go in the back room."

"This is beginning to sound serious."

They both enter the back room and Salim asks Tahir, "How do you feel about Izzat Zimam?"

"You know how I feel about Izzat. What are you driving at, Salim?"

"I met someone today who has a dear friend being held in Harbush Prison on a misdemeanor that somehow got out of hand. He knows escape is not the right way to resolve this issue. He went on to say he thought the best way out was to get him transferred from Harbush to some other prison, even if that prison happens to be Evin Prison. You know Izzat as well as anyone. He has to have something in his history that we could hang him on. If we can find something, anything, to hang over his head to use as leverage to transfer this person out of Harbush, we would be doing a great service."

"I'll do what I can. We can start by giving me the names of the people involved."

"The name of the gentleman I met today is Sulayman Azzawi. He said most people call him Sully. His friend's name being held in Hatbush is Roman Hawk."

"I want to say right off that I don't intend to be the one who will be in direct contact with Izzat with whatever I happen to find on him. That should be your new friend, Sully."

"I am sure he understands that."

"I'll do a little investigating, Salim, and will let you know what I find out."

"On behalf of my newfound friend, Sully, I thank you so much, Tahir!"

"Don't thank me now, Salim. Thank me when I have something for you. I'll be in touch."

They both give a parting wave.

Chapter Sixteen

Tuesday – May 22, 2018

12:05 P.M. Tahir walks into Salim's diner, smiling ear to ear. "Let's go into the back room. What I have is too hot for general knowledge. Salim, I hit the jackpot, as they say in America. I looked into Izzat's accounts at the bank and found that he has held two accounts; one that he uses for Harbush official business and one for his own personal use. That in itself is not unusual, but what I saw happening, the government of Iran I am sure would like to know. I didn't look at all past year's records, but during the past year, he has been taking out ten percent of what the government allows for Harbush expenses and transferring it into his personal account. I am sure the government would give anything to know that."

"That certainly is great news, and you did it so quickly, too. Let me congratulate you, Tahir. I am sure Sully would like to thank you, too. As a matter of fact, he is due here any minute. He's been checking in with me every day and having lunch about this time."

Salim and Tahir walk back into the main dining area and meet Sully as he enters the café.

Salim walks over to greet Sully. "Sully, you are just in time. I'd like you to meet the President of Bushehr National Bank, Tahir Maruf."

Sully and Tahir shake hands as Sully says, "It's a pleasure to meet you, sir!"

And Tahir adds, "It's a pleasure to meet you, as well. Let's all go back to the back room. What I have for Sully is for Sully alone."

Tahir leads off, "Sully, I was asked by Salim on your behalf, to find something on Izzat Zimam, well known beast and head of Harbush Prison. I did a little digging the last couple of days and found that for the past year, Izzat has been taking ten percent of what the government officially gives him every month to run and maintain the prison and transferring it into his own private account. What do you think the government would do to Izzat if they found that out? He would most likely spend the rest of his life in his own prison, but not as the head warden and commandant of the prison. Fellow prisoners would make it hell on earth for him."

Sully adds, "That is excellent information to have. I can't thank you enough, Mister President."

"Sully, please call me Tahir. I just want to add one minor thing. What you do with this information is up to you; just keep any reference to me out of it."

"I certainly will, Mister…I mean, Tahir!"

Then turning to Salim, he said, "I won't be confronting Izzat with this information in his prison. I might not ever make it out of Harbush. Salim, you mentioned once that Izzat comes in here to eat every so often. How often would that be?"

"I would say about every two or three weeks, and it could be any day now."

"Do you have any objection to me confronting him here in your diner, Salim?"

"As long as it's words being thrown back and forth and not fists!"

Thursday – May 24, 2018

12:26 P.M. Sully has been camped in Salim's diner from opening in the morning 'til closing at night for the last couple of days waiting and hoping that at some point he would be on hand when Izzat poked his head through the front door. As Izzat enters the diner, Salim, standing behind the counter, nods his head, signaling to Sully, *"Here's your man."*

Izzat finds a seat at a faraway table and sits down. Sully, who is holding a cup of tea, waits for him to order and then approaches Izzat, asking, "May I buy you a cup of tea?" He would have offered to buy him something stronger, except for the fact that alcohol is illegal in Iran.

Izzat retorts, "I just ordered tea, and who are you?"

"I happen to be a very dear friend of someone you are holding in that hell hole you call a prison. He was sent there for a misdemeanor that happened eight years ago, and in some way, the charge was magnified."

"That is no concern of mine. I'm not responsible for the people that are sent to me."

"You are quite right, but a kind word from you would be enough to get him transferred out of Harbush; say, to a place like Evin Prison in Tehran."

"I still don't know who you are, but you are some kind of idiot to think I would do anything like that."

"Oh, I think maybe you will. You see, I happen to have incontrovertible evidence on you that the government of Iran I am sure would love to know."

"You are bluffing! You don't have anything."

"Oh, really! I happen to know at least for the past year, you have been taking ten percent of what the government officially gives you to run and maintain Harbush Prison and depositing it into your own personal account, and I can prove it. I would say you have been very naughty, Izzat."

"How did you obtain this information? That information is supposed to be confidential."

"It doesn't matter how I obtained it. All I have to do is leak it to the right people, Izzat, and you could find yourself back in Harbush Prison serving life at hard labor. And I'm sure your fellow prisoners would just love to see you. If the guards can't inflict enough punishment on you, I am sure your fellow inmates will make up for it."

"What's your name?"

"My name is of no consequence. The name you have to remember is Roman Hawk. He arrived in that abyss you call a prison a week ago. You are going to take action to see that he is immediately transferred out of Harbush and sent to Evin Prison. I don't care what reason you give, just make it good. I'll be checking for Roman Hawk in Evin Prison in a couple of days. If I ask to see him and he is not there, you can be sure the information I have will reach the right person."

Right about now Izzat is beginning to sweat little bullets. "Alright, alright, I will do it. I just don't know if I can do it in two days."

"Of course you can! I'm being easy on you. You could do it this afternoon if you put your mind to it. Merely have your secretary type out a letter explaining the reason for his transfer and send it along with the guards driving Roman Hawk to Evin Prison. On the way, you can call Evin Prison to expect a new prisoner. It's that simple."

"What reason do I give?"

"Think of one!"

With that, Sully gets up and walks out, leaving a note of thanks on the counter with Salim.

Chapter Seventeen

Friday – May 25, 2018

6:52 A.M. Roman and John Rivers have finished breakfast and are lined up to begin receiving axes for the day's work ahead. One of the guards comes over to Roman and pulls him out of the line and says, "Come with me!"

Roman glances at John with a quizzical look as he is pulled out of line, wondering, *What have I done now?*

The guards shove Roman into the Commandant's office, and Roman stands there looking at Izzat asking himself, *Now what?*

"Roman Hawk, I had the guards bring you here so that I could inform you that you are being transferred to Evin Prison in Tehran." Izzat hands the guards an envelope containing written orders for his transfer and orders the guards. "Take this prisoner to Evin Prison in Tehran." Then he addresses Roman, "You must have friends in high places to obtain your transfer out of here. I have been the Commandant of Harbush for over twenty years, and I have never had this happen before. Handcuff him and get him out of here!"

Roman is ecstatic over leaving Harbush, but at the same time is sad that he is leaving without having a chance to say goodbye to his friend, John Rivers. As the van carrying Roman passes the bus loading prisoners for the day's labor, Roman and John catch each other's eye briefly, both wondering at that moment if they will ever see each other again.

• • • • •

3:42 P.M. The van carrying Roman arrives at the special prisoners' entrance. The warden for Evin Prison is there to meet the van. As Roman and the two guards exit the van, the warden tells them, "You can remove the handcuffs and shackles now. He's not going anywhere."

The two guards rejoin together. "We're just glad to get him off our hands."

"Did he cause you any trouble?"

"No, but we heard at Harbush that he is supposed to be some kind of killing machine. It was said that his fists are lethal weapons. That's the principal reason he is in handcuffs and shackles."

"Well, we have a way of taking care of prisoners like that."

"Would you please sign this form acknowledging your formal receipt of the prisoner?"

The warden signs the form and the guards say, "He's all yours, Warden, and good luck."

The warden is not alone with Roman Hawk. He has two hefty prison guards with him. All three escort Roman to a room where he is stripped of his clothes, shoved into a shower stall, and ordered to take a shower, which Roman was only too happy to take, his first in over a week, not counting that hosing he got after his first day of chopping down trees. After five minutes, Roman is pulled out of the shower, handed a prison uniform, ordered to put it on, and then led to a cell to share with three others. After he is shoved inside and hears the loud clank of the door closing behind him, Roman begins warily eying about trying to mentally examine each of his cellmates. He knows if he had to, he could take on all three and have 'em lying flat on the floor before they knew what hit 'em, but that would be the last thing I would want to do. That would really complicate matters. *Now that I'm here in the same prison as the Prime Minister, I have to be free as I can be to try and locate him.* Finally, one of the three approaches Roman, offering his hand in friendship.

"My name is Humam Shalah! The two sitting on the bunk are Ibrahim Hikmat and Ghazi Mahmud." They both shake hands and Roman counters with, "And my name is Roman Hawk. Good to meet all of you! How long have each of you been guests of Evin Prison?"

Ghazi Mahmud bursts out laughing, "Guests? That's a hot one! Nobody's a guest here. If I was a guest, I'd tell them where they could go and leave. How about you? What brought you here to this hell hole?"

"I just spent a week in Harbush and somehow managed to get transferred here."

All three counter with, "You were in Harbush?"

Humam has a hard time believing that and says, "Nobody ever gets out of Harbush. Being sent there is like being sentenced to a slow death and you got transferred out after only a week? That's really hard to believe."

"I know it is, but that's what happened!"

Humam again adds, "You must really have friends in high places. If you know who your friend is, ask him to do what he can to spring you from this God-forsaken place."

"How long have you all been in Evin Prison?"

"We got in late last night. We were all picked up for protesting. We all got a year at hard labor. Most likely we will start our hard labor tomorrow."

"Most likely I will be joining you tomorrow."

"How long are you in for?"

"You guys will be free long before I will. I'm due to be stuck here for fifteen years at hard labor, but better here than at Harbush."

"We hear this place is no picnic, either."

"I think you are right."

Just then five cell doors begin to automatically open. Roman asks, "What's going on?"

Humam Shalah says, "I'm not sure, but it must be our time to get some exercise in the compound."

About twenty guards show up with rifles and shot guns at the ready, shouting, "Move, move! You have one hour."

In the compound, Roman begins looking carefully at the sixteen other prisoners, hoping to luckily spot the Prime Minister. Instead, he sees several inmates approaching him, and they don't appear to be smiling. The ringleader of the five steps up to Roman. "Who are you?"

"I'm Roman Hawk, who are you?"

"You're new here, aren't you? I've never seen you before."

"I've never seen you before, either. What's your name?"

"Zuhayr Zubaydi, and you better remember it."

"You just have me shakin' all over, Zuhayr."

"You just watch your step. I've got my eye on you."

"And you can bet your bottom rival I have my eye on you."

Roman goes to sleep that night, wondering how and when he will ever meet up with the Prime Minister.

Chapter Eighteen

Saturday – May 26, 2018

6:55 A.M. Roman, along with his new cellmates and sixty others, are ordered into the back end of a number of empty dump trucks. A guard with a shot gun sits on top of the cab, facing the prisoners in the back. In addition, there are a number of cars carrying guards driving along with the caravan. The caravan drives about twenty-five miles out of Tehran to a stone quarry. One truck at a time empties its prisoners, and each prisoner is handed a sledgehammer, then ordered into the quarry to start making big stones into little ones. A pile is formed of the smaller stones and then thrown into one of the empty dump trucks.

All the while Roman is wielding away with his sledgehammer, he is scouting the area in search of the Prime Minister. Then, out of the corner of his eye, he spots someone maybe three hundred feet away that looks like it could be the Prime Minister. Carrying his sledgehammer, Roman begins to make his way toward the person he believes to be the Prime Minister. Then a guard, a few feet away, barks, "Where do you think you are going, Hawk?"

Pointing in the direction of the Prime Minister, he says, "The stones look a lot larger over there."

"Okay, Hawk, you can go where you want, but I'm keeping my eye on you."

Still shackled at the ankles, Roman slowly makes his way toward the one person he believes is the Prime Minister. Moving ever closer, Roman is convinced it is the Prime Minister.

Why on earth do they have the Prime Minister of Israel out here breaking rocks with a sledgehammer? I wonder if I can get close enough to make contact with him in some way. I won't be able to talk to him. Somehow, I will have to write out something tonight and get close enough to him tomorrow to pass it on.

• • • • •

9:36 A.M. Sully drops in at the Tehran Furniture and Storage Company and asks to see the manager. A minute or two later, Azira steps out of her office with a smile on her face.

"Sully, it's good to see you! I hope you have good news."

"I do! Roman has been transferred from Harbush Prison to Evin Prison. There was no way that I could possibly free him all together, but at least he is free of that hell-hole, Harbush."

Rina, sitting in Azira's office, heard every word and rushes out screaming, "Oh, thank you, thank you, Sully!" then runs over and gives him a big kiss on his cheek. "You don't know how relieved I am. How did you do it?"

"The first thing I did was start up a friendship with the owner of a diner in Bushehr who is a long-time resident and knows a lot of influential people in the city, including the President of Bushehr National Bank. He was also aware of Harbush Commandant, Izzat Zimam's reputation of being anything but honest. It didn't take much to put two and two together. My diner friend, Salim, explained the situation to his friend the bank president, who spent some time investigating Izzat's bank accounts and found out he was withdrawing ten percent of what Iran was paying him to maintain his prison and depositing it into his personal account. That information was passed on to me, and I confronted Izzat with it. He had no choice. He had to do what I told him to do. There was no official way that Roman could be set free, but his transfer was entirely possible."

Excitedly, Rina exclaims, "I'm going to Evin Prison tonight to see Roman. Is there anything that either of you would like me to pass on to him?"

Azira says, "Just tell him how happy we are that he is no longer under the thumb of Izzat Zimam."

· · · · ·

7:36 P.M. Rina has just undergone the visitors' inquisition at Evin Prison to see Roman and is now sitting behind a long table with glass interrupting any personal contact with the prisoner on the other side, pretty much on a par with a bank teller's window. Rina waits for Roman to appear and jumps for joy when she sees him walk through the visitor's room door.

"Oh, Roman, I can't tell you how happy I am to see you!"

"Rina, I love you! Your presence here is a like a breath of fresh spring air. I miss you so very much."

"You know how much I love you and miss you. I am lost without you."

"Just hang tough, Rina! Don't give up hope."

Having been a prisoner here once herself, she knows that every word that is said is overheard and recorded. Knowing this, Rina has written a note on a small piece of paper and surreptitiously slipped it under the glass when the nearest guard turned to watch another couple. Roman quickly picks it up and slips it into his pants pocket.

Rina asks, "What did you do today?"

"They have me on a work detail splitting rocks. It's the hard labor portion of my sentence. I would rather be doing that than just sitting in my cell, but the best thing is I am certain I saw the PM today."

"Are you sure?"

"Yes, definitely!"

Another five minutes passes by quickly, and Rina is told her time is up.

"I'll be back tomorrow, Roman, at this same time."

Roman replies, "Until tomorrow! I love you!"

Roman is frisked as he leaves the visitors room, and the note in his pocket is not detected. Back in his cell, Roman reads the note left by Rina.

It says, "I will be returning. Please jot down anything I can do to help you,"

Roman begins thinking, *"I can use this paper to help make contact with the Prime Minister. I wish Rina could have left me a pen or pencil. I've got to find one some way!*

Roman turns to Ghazi, "Do you know where I can find a pencil?"

As Ghazi wonders what he could do for Roman, Roman wildly begins thinking, *For the lack of a pencil, perhaps a Prime Minister and, in turn an illustrious nation, are to suffer a great loss. What am I thinking? I'll find a pencil somewhere. They can't be that scarce.*

Chapter Nineteen

Sunday – May 27, 2018

9:16 A.M. In the Arabic world, Sunday is just another working day, and today Roman has managed to work his way four or five feet away from the Prime Minister as they both busily split rocks. Roman waits for the nearest guard to direct his attention to several inmates in the opposite direction and begins thinking to himself, *I know their punishment for talking is harsh, but I have to take that chance.*

While continuing to break rocks, Roman whispers, "Mister Prime Minister, my name is Roman Hawk, and I am here to try to help you escape."

The Prime Minister is shocked by what he has just heard and doesn't know whether to believe Roman or not and looks very skeptically at Roman.

The guard directs his attention to Roman and the Prime Minister, and not another word is spoken that day.

· · · · ·

10:38 A.M. While Roman and the Prime Minister are breaking rocks, Rina, Azira, and Sully are in Azira's office discussing how they can aid Roman and the Prime Minister in escaping from Evin Prison.

Sully leads off, "The key to helping them both escape is to take advantage of any situation that arises while they are out of Evin Prison on work detail.

We will have to subtly follow the work detail to see where they end up. Wherever they happen to be working, they will have to work their way to the edge closest to our escape vehicle. If they are in a stone quarry breaking rocks, it may be very difficult to make their way to any edge to escape. We will have to plan it so that they make their escape before they enter the quarry. I believe it will be the only way. I will have to create some sort of diversion to direct every guard's attention away from Roman and the Prime Minister as they run to the escape vehicle. It will be difficult for them because they will be shackled as they run."

Rina asks, "What kind of diversion do you plan on using, Sully?"

"I'll create a massive explosion. It won't be hard to do. One of the things that is taught when I was undergoing CIA training was how to make powerful explosives from everyday chemicals that can be purchased at any hardware store or pharmacy. But then also realize the explosion, for the most part, will only be a very temporary diversion. It will require fast action on our part." Then Sully turns to Azira. "Azira, do you have a fast car?"

"It's a BMW!"

"That should be a good getaway car. Somehow, we will have to hide the car as close to our point of escape as we can. Once we make our escape, we will have to have some place to hide him 'til things cool down."

Azira claims, "They can hide out back in the warehouse. Nobody will find them back there."

"That sounds good, Azira! I know there is a huge element of risk in all of this, but as I see it, it is our only way. Let's plan to meet here every day at this time to briefly update ourselves to latest conditions and any changes that need to be made to our plans. In the meantime, I'm going to drive out to the quarry this afternoon and get there sometime before they leave. I want to see how many vehicles and guards are involved and get the lay of the land. I'll see you tomorrow and tell you what I find out."

Everyone agrees to meet at this time every day.

• • • • •

4:46 P.M. Sully has driven to a good spot and has taken a position on the side of the main road two or three hundred yards or so from the side road that leads to the quarry.

This looks like a good spot. The bushes on the side of the road here are help masking my position and I am far enough away that no one is going to notice me, except for a stray car driving by. Hopefully, it won't be a police car. I'm just guessing they will quit work splitting rocks around five o'clock.

At five-fifteen, Sully sees two lead vehicles and four trucks pull out of the side road, one filled with stones and the other three loaded with prisoners. A seventh vehicle, a small sedan, with guards, brings up the rear.

Sully pulls on to the main road, and keeping out of sight, follows the caravan back to Evin Prison. Again, keeping out of sight, he observes the trucks unloading prisoners and sees Roman leaving one truck and the Prime Minister leaving another.

Monday – May 28, 2018

10:30 A.M. Sully, Azira, and Rina are gathered in Azira's office.

Sully leads off, "I got a good look at the work detail as it left the quarry yesterday. It left with two, large sedans in front of four dump trucks; three loaded with prisoners and one with stones. A seventh vehicle, a small sedan, brought up the rear. I would estimate that the small sedan held no more than four guards. Since yesterday when we met, I have developed a different plan. Azira, do you have a heavy rifle with a silencer?"

"Yes, as a matter of fact, I do."

"Good! I believe what we have to do is create a blow out in the tire of the truck carrying Roman and the Prime Minister. I intend to create this blowout by shooting a hole into the side of the truck tire carrying them. This is all going to take exact timing and coordination by the three of us. It's going to be risky, but I believe it can be done. First and foremost, for it to work, Roman and the Prime Minister have to be in the same truck. Rina, it will be your job to some way get word to Roman when you see him tonight that he and the Prime Minister must get in the same truck every day. The day we pull this off, Rina, you will have to be in a position to tell me which truck they are both in. Count on the phones being tapped, so when you call, all have to say is the word, 'first,' 'second,' 'third,' or 'fourth.' That way I'll know which truck to hit. Azira, you will be standing by with the getaway car very close to where all this will happen. I will have to pick out the spot tomorrow. The small sedan in the rear with four guards is the one real obstacle that will give us trouble. I will have a rifle to use; with a silencer, no less."

Azira returns with, "I have a small arsenal locked up in the warehouse. I have whatever we need, and I will be on hand with another rifle with a silencer. Between the two of us, we will take care of the rear sedan."

Sully adds, "The timing of that has to be right, too. Rina, you have a big job in this whole thing. When the blowout occurs, I am sure a couple of prisoners will be told to change the tire. Those two prisoners have to be Roman and the Prime Minister,"

Rina remarks, "I will right all this down on paper tonight and slip it to Roman unnoticed somehow. Working together in the past, we have always managed to work out some sort of code language we could use. I'll work out something on paper and try to slip it to Roman tonight."

Sully ends by saying, "Great; then we all know what to do. Let's meet again tomorrow to begin firming things up. Tomorrow I will scout the road leading to the quarry and pick out a spot that will be best to hide your car, Azira, so it will be hidden, but close to the scene of action."

That afternoon Rina is at the desk in her room, trying to put on paper what she needs to tell Roman what to do that night.

Rina writes,

Roman, remember when we were planning breakfast for you and my minister? It was the same day that you and the minister drove home trucking vegetables together from the farm in California. We had quite a blow out that day. You and my minister had quite a good time taking part in the party.

That night Rina hands Roman the note. Back in his cell, he begins deciphering the note by circling the right words. He proceeds as follows: "Roman, remember when we were (planning) (break)fast (for) (you) and my (minister). It was the same day that (you) (and) the (minister) drove home (truck) vegetables (together) from the farm in California. We had quite a (blow out) that day. (You) (and) my (minister) had quite a good time (taking) (part) in that party.

Roman sits back and begins to put some sense into what he has circled: "Rina and perhaps Azira are planning some sort of break for me and the Prime Minister. Trucking together must mean we should be in the same truck when this break happens. I am not sure what is meant by the words 'blow out,' unless they plan on creating a blow out in one of the truck tires. And when that happens, the Prime Minister and I are to take part in changing the tire. Sounds like a good plan if they can carry it off. I've got to pass on this information to the Prime Minister. Luckily, I found this pencil stub lying on the floor of the mess hall. I'll write on the back, 'Friend planning break. Stick close to me the next few days. After reading, tear up paper into fine confetti.'"

Tuesday – May 29, 2018

6:36 A.M. Roman has managed to seek out the Prime Minister at breakfast and sits down next to him. Prisoners are allowed to talk while eating, but every word said is carefully guarded as guards are close by hearing every word.

Roman leads off, "Ira. I know who you are, sir. I met you briefly on Sunday in the stone quarry. My name is Roman Hawk, and I have allowed myself to taken prisoner to be here next to you. You must believe that! Aaron Levy knows me personally and asked me for help."

"You know Aaron Levy?"

"Yes, for eight years! He has asked for my help a number of times."

At that moment, there is a minor disturbance in another part of the mess hall that attracted the local guard's attention. During the moment, Roman furtively slips the note written the night before under the table to the Prime Minister.

Roman then remarks, "For your benefit, Ira, please believe me!"

From that point on, nothing is said.

Chapter Twenty

Tuesday – May 29, 2018

7:38 A.M. Sully is in the rear, trailing the work detail caravan about a half mile or so, and he spots an area of the road that has ideal vegetation nearby; trees and bushes, fairly close to the road, just right for hiding the get-away car. He also notes, *And it's not that far from Tehran. I'd say five or six miles. We wouldn't have too far to travel to get to Azira's warehouse. Time to turn around and head back. Mustn't miss our ten-thirty meeting.*

· · · · ·

10:30 A.M. Rina, Azira and Sully are all alone sitting in Azira's office when Sully starts off, "I believe I have found the perfect spot for hiding the get-away car, Azira. It's about five miles out of Tehran, and it is loaded with enough vegetation to easily hide your car. Would you be able to leave the office for about an hour? I'll show you the spot. I want you to be satisfied."

"Yes, I have nothing pressing at the moment."

"Okay, then, let's tentatively plan on carrying this out tomorrow. Let's meet again this afternoon at five to firm it up. Rina, if it's firmed up this afternoon, you will have to inform Roman in some way this evening that the break will happen tomorrow morning around seven-thirty."

"That could be a little difficult in terms of calling out the time, but I will do my best."

"I can't think of anything else at the moment. Are there any questions?"

No one answers! "Okay, let's meet back here at five. Azira, show me your BMW!"

"It's parked out in back of the warehouse."

"While I think of it, show me your arsenal of weapons."

"It is also toward the rear of the warehouse."

They reach the rear of the warehouse, and Azira proudly remarks, "Here it is!" She unlocks the door and turns on the light.

Overwhelmed, Sully says, "You have enough here to start a war." Then, studying to see what they could use tomorrow, Sully remarks, "These M-1 Carbines look good. I see you have them modified to accept silencers. Terrific!"

Azira adds, "I also have a couple of Uzi's that have silencers, as well."

"Good. We may need those tomorrow, as well. I'll plan on knocking on your company front door tomorrow at five-thirty. You can give me an M-1 Carbine with a silencer and an Uzi with silencer at that time. Okay, Azira, give me a BMW test drive, and I'll show you the spot I had picked out."

Within minutes, they reach the area that Sully had picked out.

"As you can see, Azira, the areas on both sides of the road have plenty of vegetation to mask our presence. But the one thing we have to watch tomorrow is that we don't end up facing one another. Neither of us want to get hurt in the crossfire."

"The area looks very good, Sully. You did a good job!"

"The best way to handle this tomorrow is to wait until Roman and the Prime Minister are well on their way to changing the tire. While this is happening, the rest of the caravan either may not notice what is happening if Roman and the Prime Minister are in the last truck, or if they happen to be in the lead truck, chances are the rest of the caravan won't sit around waiting, while a tire is being changed. In either event, I intend to wait 'til the trucks not involved, drive on to the quarry and are out of sight, before killing the guards in the rear sedan. Don't you fire until I do."

"Understood; but what if the whole caravan does wait until the tire is changed?"

"Then we don't do anything. The two of us cannot realistically take on forty or fifty guards and expect to come out on top, even with Uzi's. I really don't think that will be the case. Let's plan on getting here close to six-thirty. I estimate they will hit this spot sometime between seven and seven-thirty. Okay, Azira, let's head back."

• • • • •

5:00 P.M. Rina, Azira, and Sully are gathered together in Azira's office for one last time, as Sully leads off, "I believe we are ready to go for tomorrow. Rina, you have the all-important job tonight when you see Roman to inform him that the break will take place tomorrow morning. Also, tell him he needs to get into the last truck, if at all possible. Then tomorrow morning you have to be in position by six-thirty to determine which truck Roman and the Prime Minister will be in. Have you picked out a good spot for this?"

"Yes, I will be standing on the street corner, maybe three hundred feet away, where I will have a clear view of the whole loading operation. We are fortunate that Evin Prison is located in the heart of a Tehran residential area. The loading is out in the open."

"Okay, it sounds like we are all set. Good luck tonight, Rina, and Azira, you'll see me at six tomorrow morning."

7:35 P.M. Rina stands up and greets Roman as he enters the visitors' room and throws him a kiss. "How are you holding up, Roman?"

"I'm doing fine, Rina. There is no need to worry."

"You look a little thin. Are they feeding you well?"

"They are feeding quite fine, Rina. You needn't worry."

"I'm not sure I believe you. For example, what do you think they are planning for breakfast tomorrow?"

That question tells me only one thing. Rina and Azira are planning the break for tomorrow. Other than causing a tire blowout of the truck carrying the Prime Minister and myself, how do they intend to carry this thing off? Rina never does anything haphazardly. I am sure it is well planned out.

"I have no idea what they are planning for breakfast tomorrow. I understand your concern, but they are feeding me quite well."

"We always ate well on my parents' farm. With fifty acres of farmland, we always had plenty of food in the house. Dad insisted on having the best farm equipment. I remember he bought the last Ford truck in town. Mom thought he was crazy, but he insisted in getting the last truck. They were sometimes at odds with one another, but they still loved each other. I'm sure you understand."

"I understand what you are saying. My parents were the same way, always at odds with one another."

At that moment, a guard close by came over to tell Rina, "Your time is up, ma'am!"

Rina throws Roman another kiss. "See you tomorrow, Roman!"

Roman returns to his cell thinking, *The break is planned for tomorrow morning, and the Prime Minister and I are to get into the last truck. The Prime Minister has been sticking pretty close to me the last day or so. I shouldn't have to tell him to get into the last truck with me."*

Chapter Twenty-One

Wednesday – May 30, 2018

6:00 A.M. Azira hears Sully knocking on her front door.

"Come in, Sully, I'm ready to go. My car is out in back. We have quite a day in front of us. It gives me chills just to think about it."

"I have the good feeling that we are going to do just fine. We all know what to do; hopefully, that includes Roman and the Prime Minister, so it merely means carrying out in detail everything we had planned. Have you ever had an occasion to do anything like this before?"

"I honestly have to say, no, I haven't. Up 'til now, most of my time in Iran has been spent gathering intelligence."

Azira opens up her arsenal of weapons, and Sully comments, "Well, for someone whose primary mission is to gather intelligence, you certainly come prepared for war."

Azira and Sully pick up their M-1s and Uzis and head out to their appointed spot.

• • • • •

BACK IN EVIN PRISON

6:32 A.M. Roman and the Prime Minister are eating breakfast, as Roman comments, "Stick very close to me today, Ira."

Minutes later the prisoners begin loading into the dump trucks. Rina has taken her position across and down the street a few hundred feet but is in full view of what prisoners are loaded into what trucks.

One of the guards in charge of the loading has taken particular notice of Roman and the Prime Minister. "You two look like you are getting a little too chummy with one another. Kaplan, you get in the lead truck, and Hawk, you get in the last truck."

Rina sees what is happening and desperately begins thinking, *Oh, my God! This is terrible! They're not getting into the same truck. There is no way that Sully and Azira can save both of them now. Sully instructed to call out the truck position by just the number in the caravan, lead truck as number one. If I call out one and four, he has no way of knowing who is in which truck. Under the circumstances, I could just call out 'Kaplan in one!' That might save the Prime Minister, but it would leave Roman with the present option of serving the next fifteen years in Evin Prison. The Prime Minister hasn't been brought up for trial yet. We could plan for his escape sometime while he is outside of Evin Prison. I doubt if we could use the 'blowout' ruse again to save Roman. I don't want to save just the Prime Minister; we need to save Roman, too. I'm calling Sully with number four."*

• • • • •

6:47 A.M. Sully and Azira have taken positions on opposite sides of the road but out of each other's crossfire. Both are well hidden by trees, bushes, and underbrush, and both are armed with an M-1 Carbine rifle with silencer, as well as an Uzi with silencer. They sit and wait for just the right moment.

• • • • •

7:42 A.M. Sully and Azira begin to hear the rumble of trucks in the distance. Azira quivers a little at the thought of what is about to happen. Sully's phone rings, and he hears Rina's voice as she calls out, "Number four!"

The lead cars carrying the guards pass by. Then, as the trucks pass by, Sully counts one, two, three. When truck number four reaches him, he fires at the rear tire, which explodes as the bullet pierces through the side wall. The truck comes to a screeching halt. Sully immediately observes there is no rear sedan in the caravan today. *That is going to make things a lot easier.*

A guard inside the cab of the truck gets out to check what happened and shouts to the guard sitting on top of the cab, "One of the rear tires has had a blowout. Have a couple of prisoners in the truck change the tire."

Two prisoners are ordered out to change the tire. Roman is the first to volunteer. When Sully sees Roman jump out without the Prime Minister, he begins wondering what type of action he should take. *I don't know which truck the Prime Minister is in, or if he is actually in any of them.*

The lead cars and the other three trucks stop momentarily, then proceed on to the stone quarry just as Sully suspected they would. Roman and the other prisoner are still looking for tools when Sully sees the caravan drive out of sight.

About this time, Sully pulls out his M-1 Carbine and shoots the guard sitting on the cab, just wounding him. The guard leans over and sits there, unconscious for several seconds before falling over and dropping into the rear of the truck holding twenty prisoners. While this is happening, Azira races out from her position of hiding and tells Roman and Sully, "Come on, jump in!"

As Azira speeds off, prisoners begin jumping out of the truck and running in all directions. The two guards in the cab jump out and begin firing in the direction of escaping prisoners and only wounding a couple.

All of this took place without the guards in the leading vehicles or the following three trucks aware of what happened.

Sully looks at Roman sitting in the back and asks, "How are you, Roman? Do you need any medical attention?"

"I'm fine, Sully! It's good to see some friendly faces. Between Harbush and Evin, it's great to walking free again, even if I do have to be looking over my shoulder. Where is Rina right now?"

Azira responds, "She should be meeting us when we get to my office."

On the way back, Azira remarks, "I thought we might have to change cars, so I slapped on fake license plates."

Sully looks over at Azira. "The only person alive that could identify this getaway car is the guard sitting on the cab roof, and he fell into rear of the truck unconscious. Roman, can you tell us what happened to the Prime Minister? I'm dying to know."

"Sure, during the loading process, the Prime Minister and I were about to enter into the last truck when a guard approached us and said, 'You two are getting too close to one another. I need to split you up, so he put the Prime Minister in the lead truck and me in the rear truck.'"

"So, the Prime Minister was in the leading truck. Very interesting."

$$\bullet \quad \bullet \quad \bullet \quad \bullet \quad \bullet$$

8:52 A.M. As Sully, Azira, and Roman enter Azira's office, Rina is already there waiting for them. Rina and Roman run to each other's arms and spend a minute or two just enjoying being close to one another again. After a while, Sully asks Rina, "Knowing our primary mission was to save the Prime Minister, why didn't you give me his location in the number one truck?"

"That is an obvious question. The answer to me was not so obvious. I was forced into deliberating as to what would be the best overall answer. To me, the answer was saving both Roman and the Prime Minister, and not either or. I could have called out number one, and we would have saved the Prime Minister, but that would have left Roman serving a fifteen-year sentence with no exit from Evin Prison, other than getting out to break rocks in the stone quarry. I doubt seriously if today's blowout routine would have any chance of working again. On the other hand, the Prime Minister still has to stand trial affording plenty of opportunity to free him outside of Evin. I had very little time to make a choice, and I chose to save both. Prime Minister or not, I had no intention of leaving my husband behind."

A little sheepish, Sully remarks, "You did the only sensible thing, Rina! I should have anticipated that something like this could have happened. Very seldom does any perfect plan go unchallenged. Welcome home, Roman!"

"Sully, I don't how I'll ever be able to thank you for first getting me out of Harbush and then with the help of Azira, pulling off this event this morning. Wow! You're my hero! I owe a lot to everybody here."

Roman looks around the room at all three. "Because of me, the Prime Minister is still a prisoner in Evin Prison, and I am going to do all I can to see him free. Let's put our heads together to see what it will take."

Sully comments, "Well, I doubt seriously if we can use the old blowout routine again. They will be well prepared for that type of event again, driving to the stone quarry."

Rina counters with, "It wouldn't have to be the stone quarry that frees him from Evin Prison for a while. He still has a trial on his schedule. Maybe we could strong arm the guards as he exits Evin or the courthouse after a trial day."

Roman remarks, "That could possibly work, but it's still a little iffy depending on who else is around at the time."

Rina remarks, "Roman, I've never known you to be so extra cautious."

"We have the Prime Minister's life at stake, and what we plan must eliminate any unforeseen chances. I suggest we stake out the route taken by the car carrying the Prime Minster to and from the courthouse to give us the best spot to set him free, then decide what action to take."

Sully says, "I whole heartedly agree! And I have the car to use."

Chapter Twenty-Two

Monday – June 4, 2018

On Friday, June 1, the papers headlined the news that the trial of the Prime Minister of Israel will begin on Monday, June 4.

· · · · ·

6:45 A.M. Sully has taken a position several hundred feet from the prison's exit for prisoners.

· · · · ·

8:26 A.M. Sully sees the exit door open and the Prime Minister dressed in an elegant looking business suit is escorted out the door in handcuffs and without the shackles. A guard on either side of him sees him into a waiting car. In addition, a motorcycle escort is provided for the journey to the courthouse; one in front of the Prime Minister's car and one following in back.

Sully follows the Prime Ministers car the entire route to the courthouse well behind them so as not to be noticed, and at the same time studying the areas enroute for the best spot to free him.

Sully takes a seat at the rear of the courtroom and waits for the proceedings to begin.

•   •   •   •   •

9:00 A.M. The judge appearing in civilian clothes enters the courtroom, and the bailiff cries out, "All rise!" There are no jurors, just a judge, a prosecutor, a defense counsel, a stenographer to record the proceedings, and the Prime Minister standing on a small platform with a guard on either side of him.

The prosecutor leads off with a short, opening statement: "Your honor, the Prime Minister of Israel in court today is accused of ordering the destruction of half of Iran's precious oil fields, the life blood of our economy which, in turn, is putting the lives of many Iranians in jeopardy."

Then the judge asks, "Does the defense wish to make an opening statement?"

"I do, your Honor! It is easy for the prosecutor to stand there and accuse my client of this dastardly attack on Iran, but until it is proven that Israel carried out this attack and not some other country, my client must be declared innocent."

The trial proceeded throughout the day with the prosecutor presenting witnesses who verified the bomb remnants as belonging to Israel and the defense counsel defying their credibility. At the end of the day, the judge declared, "The court is recessed until tomorrow morning at nine o'clock, so the court can deliberate its findings."

As the judge departs, the bailiff cries out, "All rise!"

At five forty-five, the Prime Minister is seen leaving the courthouse escorted by a guard on either side of him. The three enter the waiting car and again accompanied by a motorcycle escort both in front and in the rear. The small caravan of three vehicles follows the same route back that was taken in the morning, and Sully has picked out a spot that can be used to attack the Prime Minister's car.

• • • • •

7:12 P.M. Roman and Rina are still holed up in Azira's warehouse as Sully arrives in the evening. The four get together again to plot out their plan for the next day.

Sully begins, "I have picked out what I believe to be the best location. It is on the route taken this morning and again this afternoon. It is also in a lowly populated residential area, not too far from Evin Prison. Being relatively close to home base, they may have the feeling they are home free and perhaps relaxed their guard. And being low-populated lowers the odds of any civilians being hurt in the crossfire. In addition, there is a waist high type of picket fence along the sidewalk that could be used to mask the shooter's position. Now, the question is: How do we go about attacking the Prime Minister's car?"

Rina responds, "Why don't we use the blowout routine again?"

Sully adds, "I don't think they will fall for that again."

Roman speaks up, "I disagree, Sully. We can use that motorcycle escort to our advantage by picking off the one in the front and the one in the back. After we stop them with a blowout, the car will be more than likely stuck between them. It's human nature to want to determine the cause of something like a blowout, and most everyone will stop to look, including the motorcycle escort. You can count on the driver not getting out, but I would be willing to bet the guards in the back seat most likely will. Once the shooting starts, we should pick off the two escort cops first; that could very well limit the car from backing up or pulling forward. Then it's a matter of picking off the other three before they have a chance to react and see where the shots are coming from. Like most well laid plans, it may not work out exactly as described, I think it has a very good chance of working."

Azira responds, "Roman, I'll have two M-1 rifles ready for you and Rina tomorrow, and the getaway car ready to pick everyone up."

Sully remarks, "As soon as we finish here, Rina, I'll show you the spot that I picked out."

"Thanks, Sully, that sounds good."

Looking at everyone in the room, Roman asks, "Are there any last minute questions or comments?"

No one answers, then Sully turns to Rina. "Come on, Rina, I'll show you the spot I picked out."

Tuesday – June 5, 2018

10:00 A.M. The courtroom is packed with standing-room-only spectators, all tensely waiting to hear the verdict by the judge. Then, as the judge enters, a hush draws over the crowd. The bailiff cries out, "All rise!" and the judge takes his seat behind the bench. The judge then addresses the defendant, who is no longer standing on the platform when the judge initially addressed him but is seated at a table with his counsel.

"Will the defendant please rise!"

The Prime Minister, along with his defense counsel, rise to hear the verdict.

"After hearing all the evidence and arguments presented by both sides in this trial against the Prime Minister of Israel, the court finds the defendant guilty as charged and is sentenced to serve life imprisonment at hard labor. The sentence will be served at Harbush Prison. This case is now closed."

As the judge leaves the courtroom, the bailiff cries out, "All rise!"

Sully, who had taken a position in the back row, calls Rina.

"The judge just announced the verdict. Are you both in place?"

"Yes, just waiting for the right moment."

Sully is doing his best to keep an eye on the Prime Minister from what he hopes is an undetectable distance. He gets in his car and follows well behind the car carrying the Prime Minister. Then suddenly he sees the car taking a different route back to Evin Prison. *This spells trouble!* Sully follows the car a bit longer and sees it pulling into the parking lot of Tehran's main police station. *It looks like they will be holding the Prime Minister here for further transfer to Harbush Prison.*

Sully gets on the phone right away. "They have taken him to Tehran's main police station for further transfer to Harbush. Meet me at Azira's right away."

"Roman, the Prime Minister is being sent to Harbush Prison; can you believe it? Sully is calling a meeting at Azira's as soon as we can get there."

$$\bullet \quad \bullet \quad \bullet \quad \bullet \quad \bullet$$

11:34 A.M. Sully opens the conversation. "I guess you all know by now the Prime Minister is being sent to Harbush Prison. It looks like they are pulling no punches. What is our next plan of action?"

Roman leads off again, "It stands to reason that we can't let the Prime Minister reach Harbush. I know the route that was taken for me, and it goes right through Qom. I suggest we hide the car somewhere on the road between Tehran and Qom. Although they will be carrying the Prime Minister, I doubt they will make a big event over his transfer with any kind of police escort because of the great distance involved. I can't see them doing any more than using an ordinary car carrying the Prime Minister with a guard on either side of him in the back and the driver with a person riding shotgun in the front; the less conspicuous the better. I am also sure they will be heavily armed, and if it is anything like last time, they are probably on their way right now."

Sully comments, "I think you are probably right, Roman; the less conspicuous the better."

Roman continues, "It's about an eight-hour trip from Bushehr to Tehran, so I have them arriving here around seven tonight to pick up the Prime Minister and leaving the jail by seven-thirty or eight. Based on that timeline, we should be waiting for them in place on the road to Qom no later than eight. Anybody? Any thoughts on what I've said?"

Sully is the only one to respond. "I think you have covered it pretty well, Roman."

"That gives Rina and me 'til about eight tonight to find a good spot."

Chapter Twenty-Three

Tuesday – June 5, 2018

8:00 P.M. Roman and Rina are staked out on the side of the road about five miles outside of Tehran.

"This looks like a good spot, Rina. I think you had a good idea to jack up the rear end of the car to make look like we are fixing a flat. We can use the car to shield us, although I hate the thought having to return Azira's car with a few bullet holes. In a way I find it quite humorous, but it really isn't. I'm sure any body shop might have a question or two."

Wednesday – June 6, 2018

12:26 A.M. "Well, Rina, we have been here over four hours. I guess it's possible they took another route. I don't see how we could have missed them otherwise. Let's take the jack, lower the car, and head back to Azira's. It has been good of her to put us up. I'll call her and tell her we are coming back."

• • • • •

1:08 A.M. Azira is waiting for them when they arrive at the back of the warehouse, and she asks, "What happened?"

Roman responds, "We never saw the car. There is no way we could have missed it."

"Isn't it possible you could have missed it on a dark night like tonight?"

"We parked in an area where we had plenty of overhead road lights. Also, at that time of night, road travel is very light, almost non-existent, and I am familiar with the car they use. There is no way we missed them."

"What do you plan to do now?"

"Rina and I will check with Sully in the morning. Perhaps he can check with the Police Chief to see at least when they left. In the meantime, let's all get some shut eye!"

• • • • •

7:18 A.M. Sully calls Azira, "What happened last night? Did Roman and Rina manage to get the Prime Minister?"

"No, they didn't. They said they never saw the car that they believed he would be carried in. Roman had planned on calling you this morning to see if you could check with Police Chief Abbas to find out what time they left yesterday."

"I'll look into that Azira and get back to you."

• • • • •

8:28 A.M. "Could I please speak with Police Chief Abbas? Please tell him it's Sulayman Azzawi calling."

Moments later, "Good morning, Sulayman; what can I do for you this morning?"

"Good morning, Chief. Can you tell me what time the Prime Minister was picked up yesterday?"

"Anything dealing with the Prime Minister has been classified as TOP SECRET! I can't pass out any information."

"But, Chief, you know me! I work for Savama, Iranian Intelligence."

"I doubt if even Savama knows. My orders came from President Tahir al Majid himself. Apparently, he is taking no chances in anything getting out that might interfere with the Prime Minister's transfer to Harbush Prison. Sorry, Sulayman!"

"That's alright, Chief, I understand your position. Thanks, anyway!"

As soon as Sully hangs up with Police Chief Abbas, he calls Azira. "Azira, I just finished speaking with Police Chief Abbas. He was able to tell me nothing, as he received orders from none other than President Tahir al Majid himself that anything dealing with the Prime Minister was top secret. So, we have no information and won't be getting any. I think we have to assume that at this point, the Prime Minister is going to be a prisoner of Harbush. I think this calls for another meeting to see what we can do to obtain his release."

"This is horrible news. Besides passing this on to Roman and Rina, I need to relay this information on to Aaron Levy. No telling what will happen when he hears this news. Oh, here are Roman and Rina now. Hang on, Sully, while I tell them this awful news."

Azira turns to Roman and Rina. "I have Sully on the line. He just informed me that he spoke to Chief Abbas, and the Chief had orders from the President that no information was to be handed out regarding the Prime Minister. In Sully's opinion, we should assume that the Prime Minister is now a prisoner of Harbush and feels a need to set up another meeting to obtain his release."

Roman responds, "I couldn't agree more and the sooner the better."

Roman gets on Azira's phone. "When can you get here, Sully?"

"I'll be there in thirty minutes."

• • • • •

9:25 A.M. Sully, Azira, Roman, and Rina are gathered in Azira's office. Roman leads off, "I'm open to suggestions."

Sully responds, "Roman, I think it's time you and I pay a visit to my friend Salim Tilfah, who owns that small café in Bushehr and tell him we have someone else we need to free from Harbush Prison. He was only too happy to help me free you."

Roman smiles and says, "Sully, what would we do without you? What are we waiting for?"

Rina adds, "You don't intend to leave me behind, do you? This sounds like you could very well use another hand."

Roman remarks, "Rina, we had no intention of leaving you behind. You have always been the better half of our team. Azira, we are on a mission to save the Prime Minister, and with your permission, the three of us are going to unload your arsenal because I have a feeling we are going to need it."

Azira happily replies, "Go right ahead and put it to good use."

Roman, Rina, and Sully load up Sully's car with everything in Azira's arsenal and head for Bushehr.

LATER THE SAME DAY

3:20 P.M. The car carrying the Prime Minister departs from Tehran's main city jail and heads for Harbush Prison, arriving at twenty-eight minutes after midnight of Thursday, June 7. All the while, the Prime Minister is wondering, *Just what kind of HELL am I in for?*

• • • • •

12:28 A.M. The huge, mammoth, wooden gate doors open up on the Prime Minister's arrival, and the first thing that he sees is Izzat Zimam standing in front of his office, waiting to greet him. Still in handcuffs and ankle shackles, the Prime Minister labors to step out of the car. Izzat smiles and says, "You don't know how happy I am to see you tonight, Mister Prime Minister. Welcome to your own little private HELL!"

The Izzat greets the Prime Minister in the same usual manner as he does all new prisoners with a hard blow to the head with his cane. This is followed by his usual greeting: "That is just a small token of what you can expect if you get out of line. The rules of the prison are posted on the front of the building. Obey them to the letter. If you break them, I'll break you."

Then, addressing the guards, he says, "Show our new guest to his quarters."

Thursday – June 7, 2018

6:00 A.M. Gharib Taha, the prison lackey, begins ringing a bell as loudly as he can. "Roll call! Roll call! You have one minute to get out in front in line."

Gharib begins calling the roll and when he gets to the Prime Minister's name, Kaplan, there is no response. A minute later, the Prime Minister rushes out to fall in line. "Sorry if I'm late. I didn't get to bed 'til very late last night. It was a little hard to get moving this morning."

"That's too bad, Mister Prime Minister. You broke one of the prison's rules, and I'm afraid it is going to cost you. Come with me; we are going to see the Commandant."

The Prime Minister shuffles along with his shackles 'til they reach the Commandant's office. "Stand here until the Commandant arrives." Gharib departs, leaving the Prime Minister standing alone in front of the Commandant's office. Two hours later, Izzat Zimam arrives at his office to see the Prime Minister standing there. He questions, "What are you doing standing in front of my office?"

"I was told to stand here by someone who called the roll this morning."

"Did you miss roll call?"

"No, I was just a bit late."

"In other words, you broke one of the prison's rules."

"Yes, I guess so!"

"What did I tell you about breaking prison rules, Mister Prime Minister? I think you need a little reminder."

Izzat tells an assistant standing by, "Put this prisoner in the BOX for twenty-four hours." Then, addressing the Prime Minister, he says, "Because it is your first offense, the penalty is only twenty-four hours."

The box is an upright structure similar to the old telephone booth, only much smaller. There is no room to lie down or sit. There is only enough room to, more or less, stand upright for twenty-four hours with no food or water.

The Prime Minister is forced into the box, and as he stands there with hands in handcuffs and ankle shackles, he lifts up his eyes to heaven and prays, "Oh, God in heaven, give me strength!" The door is then slammed shut, leaving the Prime Minister in total darkness.

Friday – June 8, 2018

9:00 A.M. The door to the box is opened, and the Prime Minister slumps to the ground in a semi-conscious state. Two guards carry him to where he collapses down on his straw bed. He is left alone the rest of the day. He is awakened at five-thirty that afternoon when he hears the other prisoners returning from their day of wood chopping and getting the Friday hosing down. Hearing about the Prime Minister's arrival in prison, John Rivers seeks him out lying on his bed.

"Mister Prime Minister, my name is John Rivers. I have to believe that you and I are probably the only two people here that really don't belong here.

As a reporter for the *New York Globe*, I was covering a story in Turkey near the Iranian border and by mistake crossed over into Iran. I was put on trial as a spy, and here I am. I can't imagine why you are here."

"In retaliation for the bombing and killing of thousands of civilians in the Golan Heights, I ordered half of Iran's oil fields to be bombed. Then, on a mission to Turkey, my plane was shot down with surface to air missiles. I was subsequently picked up by Hezbollah helicopters and then transferred to Iran. The rest you know!"

"Come on, I'll take you to what they call dinner. Are you able to walk? I heard they put you in the box. That's about as inhumane as it gets."

"Yes, I think I can make it."

"Good, I'll tell you what you can expect for tomorrow."

Chapter Twenty-Four

Wednesday – June 6, 2018

FLASH BACK
DAY THE PRIME MINISTER IS SENT TO HARBUSH

6:18 P.M. Roman, Rina, and Sully arrive in Bushehr and pull up to Salim Til-fah's café. Sully walks in smiling and says, "Salim, I'd like you to meet some friends of mine, Roman and Rina Hawk."

Salim responds, "Any friends of Sully's are certainly friends of mine." He extends his hand and says, "It's a pleasure to meet you both."

Roman and Rina shake his hand and Roman, remarks, "Sully has told us an awful lot about you, Salim. It's almost like I know you already."

Then Sully asks, "Could we use your back room for a few minutes, Salim?"

"Yes, of course!"

"I suppose you may be wondering what brings me back here. Roman, here is the one you helped free from that hell hole called Harbush, and now I'm back with Roman to help free someone else. I am sure you have read the papers about Israel's Prime Minister being put on trial; well, he is the person we are looking to free. Roman, Rina and I are going to approach Izzat Zimam using the same information I used to get Roman transferred to Evin Prison, only it won't be used to get the Prime Minister transferred. We plan to free him, and we need to confront Izzat when he sits down in your diner. Do you have any idea when he might show up here?"

"I haven't seen him since the last time you were here. That was two weeks ago. He could be back any day now, or he may not intend to return at all after the encounter he had his last time here,

Roman looks at Sully, "Why don't we stake out Harbush's front gate to see where he goes when he leaves, then confront him wherever he takes us?"

Sully remarks, "I'll go for that! It's almost dinner time now. Maybe we'll get lucky,"

As the three are on the road to Harbush, they see Izzat drive past them, going in the opposite direction. Sully comes to a screeching halt and makes a sharp one-eighty following Izzat's car. They follow his car, only to see him park it and walk into Salim's diner. Several minutes later, Roman, Rina, and Sully enter and see Izzat seated in his usual spot. As he sees Sully approach, he starts to get up to walk out.

Sully remarks, "Izzat, there's no need for you to get up. I see this room is empty right now; that is good. My friends and I just want to have a little friendly chat with you."

Izzat looks at Roman and asks, "What the hell are you doing here? What are you doing out of Evin Prison?"

"They saw the error of their ways, Izzat, and gave me a reprieve."

"What kind of bullshit is that?

Sully continues, "My friends and I are here to discuss a business arrangement with you. You are holding another good friend of ours, Izzat, and we would like to see him released."

"You know, this is starting to become a bad habit. Alright, who are we talking about this time?"

"Probably your prime prisoner, the Prime Minister of Israel!"

"You must be out of your mind to think I would or even could have him transferred to Evin Prison."

"I don't think you understand, Izzat. We don't want him transferred. We want him freed."

"You are insane, the lot of you. One call from me and you are back in Harbush, Hawk."

Sully again remarks, "I think maybe you have forgotten I have enough provable evidence on you to throw 'you' into Harbush, and I am not the only one to have this evidence. Any tricks from you and this other person will know what to do with the evidence."

"Okay, okay, but understand I don't have the authority or jurisdiction to do what you ask!"

Roman adds, "I am sure something can be worked out. You could arrange to have the Prime Minister make an escape while out chopping wood. That way the evidence against you would remain under lock and key."

"But there would be a board of inquiry. How would I go about explaining his escape?"

"As I recall, someone once said, 'Think of something.' Which would you rather have, Izzat, a reprimand and maybe lose your job or serve time in Harbush yourself?"

"Alright, I see I don't have much of a choice. I'll have to take my chances with the board. And I'll arrange it with the guards to have him escape while out chopping wood. Of course, I'll have to pay off the guards."

Sully adds, "With what you have scared away, that should be no problem. Have the escape look real by having the guards fire shots into the air."

"It's going to take me a short time to set this whole thing up. How do I contact you?"

"How much time are we talking about?"

"Two or three days!"

"Why do you need so much time?"

"I need to discuss this with the guards and make sure they are all behind me on this. Also, we'll have to plan on how we are going to carry this off, so in the eyes of the rest of the prisoners, the escape looks real."

"Give us an exact date when you plan on carrying this out."

"Okay, I'll give you an exact date—this Saturday. Hawk knows where we have been clearing the woods. I can even give you the hour—ten in the morning."

Saturday – June 9, 2018
DAY OF THE BIG ESCAPE

Izzat has had his meeting with the guards and paid them off.

• • • • •

7:18 A.M. Roman, Rina, and Sully are seated in Salim's café having breakfast as Roman addresses Rina and Sully.

"When we get to the woods this morning, expect the worst to happen. I wouldn't be surprised to see him have a sudden change of heart and double-cross us, just be prepared for anything. I have a feeling we may need all of Azira's arsenal." And, looking at Sully, he says, "Sully, your car may take a beating today. When we are finished, I'll buy you a car of your choice."

"Don't worry about it, Roman. Whatever happens, happens. I hope we have enough of a car to drive back."

Roman looks at Rina and Sully. "It looks like we are all set; let's go."

• • • • •

9:55 A.M. Sully has parked his car on the side of the road with a full view of everyone's activity in the woods. Roman looks for the Prime Minister and sees him not too far from the road with a guard or two standing in the way. Also, in the foreground is Izzat, standing near the Prime Minister, chopping wood.

Roman's suspicious mind begins pondering, *Why is Izzat here today? This is not like him to risk his life in any way by being so close to any dangerous activity. I think maybe he has had a change of heart and is planning the old double-cross.*

Rina and Sully have taken positions behind the car as Roman gets out of the car and begins walking toward the Prime Minister. The Prime Minister sees him as Roman yells to him, "Sir, the time is now! Run to me as fast as you can."

Being shackled, the Prime Minister tries his best to run and trips on the side of the road. At the same time, Izzat gives the order to start shooting, and they do, by shooting in the air. It didn't occur to them that Izzat was actually serious about shooting the Prime Minister at this particular moment as they were paid off to do otherwise. Roman runs over, grabs the Prime Minister, and lifts him up carrying him to the car.

Roman gets about halfway to the car when Izzat grabs a pistol from one of the guards and begins shooting at Roman, getting off two rounds. Rina and Sully immediately counter with raking fire, hitting Izzat in the chest near a shoulder and his right leg. Not knowing how badly Izzat was hurt, Roman, Rina, Sully, and the Prime Minister burn rubber as they head for Tehran.

Rina looks over at the Prime Minister and cries out, "Sir, you are bleeding!"

"I think one of Izzat's bullets caught my left arm near the shoulder."

Sully stops the car suddenly and jumps out, yelling, "I have a first aid kit in the trunk of my car." Picking up the kit, he jumps back into the car, handing the kit to Roman. Roman rips open the shirt and begins soaking up the blood with large, gauze bandages.

"It looks like the bullet is still lodged in there. I can't take it out here. I will do what I can to minimize the bleeding until we get to Azira's. With my work in the FBI, I have a little practice with this type of thing before. Just hang in there, sir. You are in no danger of any permanent injury."

· · · · ·

8:41 P.M. Roman, Rina, Sully, and the Prime Minister drive up to the back of Azira's warehouse. Azira has been on pins and needles waiting for them to arrive back and hear what happened. She hears the car drive up and flies out the door to see Roman getting out.

"What happened? Did you get the Prime Minister? Are you all okay? Do you need any medical attention?"

Roman remarks, "We have the Prime Minister, but he is suffering from a bullet wound in his left arm, near the shoulder. Actually, it appears to more of a shoulder wound. Heat up some boiling water, Azira. And do you have an instrument we can sterilize by flame to withdraw the bullet; also, if you have it, an anesthetic."

"Well, you've come to the right place. Working for Aaron Levy, I have to be ready for anything."

Sitting upright in a wooden chair, Roman goes to work anesthetizing the wound, with flame-sterilized surgical, needle nose-type pliers to withdraw the bullet. Roman then stitches up the area, wipes it with sterile alcohol, and bandages the wound. Part of a large sheet is then torn to form a sling to cradle his arm.

Roman asks, "Do you have any large bolt cutters, Azira? We need to cut off his shackles. Fortunately, he wasn't handcuffed while chopping wood."

"Yes, I do! Occasionally, we also need something like that in this line of work."

Roman remarks, "Azira, you're amazing! Is there anything you don't have?"

"Yes, a gold Cadillac!"

While the Prime Minister is resting in an easy chair, Roman uses the bolt cutter to remove the Prime Minister's shackles. He heaves a big sigh of relief. "You don't know what a great feeling it is to get rid of those things."

Roman looks him square in the eye. "Yes, I do, Mister Prime Minister. I was a prisoner of Harbush myself once, not too long ago."

"You were a prisoner of Harbush? We have much in common, and I owe you, as well as everyone here, my life. Thank you all so very much!"

Roman adds, "You are not quite home free yet, Mister Prime Minister, not until you are safely out of the country. You will have to hide out here until things die down quite a bit. I am sure they are organizing an all-out, country-wide manhunt for you right now."

"How long do you think it will be necessary for me to hide out here?"

Roman responds, "I am estimating two to four weeks. Sully will let us know when the time is right."

"How do I make it out of Iran?"

Roman asks, "Do you get seasick easily, Mister Prime Minister?"

"I don't believe so! Why do you ask?"

"We will be taking a fishing boat from Now Shahr to Baku in Azerbaijan."

"Wow! That sounds exciting. And now I wish you all would do me one more favor."

They all say, "Of course, Mister Prime Minister! We would be happy to."

"Please, do not address me as 'Mister Prime Minister.' As I said earlier, I owe my life to all of you, so please, just call me Ira!"

They all reply, "Whatever you would like, Mister...Ira."

Azira remarks, "I have several, large, wooden crates that we can use if we need to...on a temporary basis, that is. I can nail the crates shut once you are inside. Of course, you will have a limited air supply, so it can only be for a short period of time. But if we can get any kind of forewarning, they will be an excellent place to hide. No one will be looking for you inside a sealed crate."

Sully mentions, "Working for Savama, I will stay up to date on how the manhunt is proceeding in Tehran. When I hear the search is closing in on this area, I will alert Azira to box you up."

Chapter Twenty-Five

Sunday – June 10, 2018

9:00 A.M. President al Majid has called an emergency meeting of everyone directly involved in the recapture of Prime Minister Kaplan. Those in attendance are Army General Zubaydi, Deputy Warden Maruf of Harbush Prison, Savama Director Yasin, and Tehran Chief of Police Abbas.

President al Majid addresses Army General Zubaydi: "General Zubaydi, I designate you in charge of this nationwide manhunt. Leave no stone unturned. Turn the country upside down if you have to but bring in Prime Minister Kaplan. If you find him and bring him in, you will be amply rewarded. If you fail, you may suffer the consequences."

• • • • •

9:45 A.M. Immediately after his first meeting, President al Majid holds a board of inquiry into the escape of Prime Minister Kaplan. In attendance are Deputy Warden Maruf and Minister of Justice Rukan.

President al Majid addresses Deputy Warden Maruf: "I realize as Deputy Warden, you did not have ultimate control of Harbush Prison, but can you shed any light on how the Prime Minister managed to escape?"

"I always told Warden and Commandant Zimam that we needed more guards on hand to oversee the labor battalion, but in his opinion, he felt we had enough. Apparently, he wanted to keep the cost of funding Harbush Prison down."

"Well, he should be commended for that. He should also be commended for his bravery and risking his life in his effort to prevent the escape of Prime Minister Kaplan. To that end, I hereby declare, in his recognition, the name Harbush Prison be renamed Zimam Prison."

President al Majid stands, followed by Deputy Warden Maruf and Minister of Justice Rukan, and all three give a hand salute.

Thursday – June 14, 2018

1:21 P.M. Azira receives a call from Sully. "Azira, I believe the police are headed your way. Time to take action."

Azira calls Roman, Rina, and the Prime Minister together and breaks out the hammer and nails. "I just had a call from Sully. It's time to jump into these crates. It shouldn't be for long. The crates are large enough, so you should have plenty of air. I even drilled some tiny holes in the sides. They are small enough not to get noticed but large enough to let in some air."

Roman says, "You are quite remarkable, Azira. Pound away!"

Azira seals up all the crates and then asks, "Are you all okay?"

They all yell back, "We're fine!"

• • • • •

2:46 P.M. One of Azira's staff hears a knock on the warehouse front door and answers it. The Tehran police identify themselves and respond, "We are conducting a search of all premises in the city for an escaped convict. I have a warrant authorizing us to do just that."

The staff member calls Azira out of her office. "Azira, the police are here to conduct a search for some missing escaped prisoner."

"Ma'am, we need to search your entire warehouse for a prisoner that escaped."

"There is no one here but me and the workers, you see, but please go ahead."

The police officers appear to be very thorough searching behind and under every large item. Finally, they reach the rear of the warehouse and observe the several large crates. They ask Azira, "What's in these crates?"

"Some fine, delicate furniture that is due to be shipped."

"Open up one of these crates."

"That's a lot of work opening one of these crates and sealing it up again."

"I'm sorry, lady, but it is necessary for us to verify."

"Alright, if you really think it is necessary."

Azira spends maybe five minutes opening up a crate. When she pulls the top off, she shows the officers that it is, indeed, filled with fine furniture.

"Okay, lady, we're convinced. Come on, Mahmud, let's check out the place next door."

Roman, Rina, and the Prime Minister could hear every word that was spoken, and when they emerged from their crates, they all said, "That was close!"

Azira answered, "Not really. I really did have a crate filled with fine furniture. I just opened it up!"

• • • • •

3:24 P.M. One of the agents from Savama Intelligence, Ayad Naqib, is questioning the guards that were on duty in the labor camp guarding prisoners the day of the Prime Minister's escape.

"You say you were standing guard the day the Prime Minister escaped, and you got a good look at the car as it sped away?"

"Yes, sir! It was a black Alfa-Romeo. I noted the license plate number first. It was 224WD53."

"That was great work! I see you are a sergeant. I'll make sure you get a promotion."

"Thank you, sir!"

Friday – June 15, 2018

8:35 A.M. Savama agent Naqib enters Savama Director Hamza Yasin's office to inform him of the information he obtained yesterday from the Harbush guard. Yasin immediately orders a quick check of Tehran license plate numbers and discovers that the car used for the Prime Minister's escape actually belongs to none other than his close associate and advisor Sulayman Azzawi. Sully is quickly called into Hamza Yasin's office.

As Sully enters Yasin's office, he is asked to have a seat.

"May I get you some coffee or tea, Sulayman?"

"No, thank you, sir!"

About this time, Sully is realizing that this is going to amount to something other than the usual call to his office.

"Sulayman, you have held a position of high honor in this organization for many years serving under Mahmud Abuzar before I assumed his position. I heard something this morning that leaves me a little confused. Actually, I can't believe what I just heard. Perhaps you may have some explanation that will make some sense. I was told this morning by one of our agents who learned from a guard the day of the Prime Minister's escape that he saw the car speeding away with the Prime Minister. He described the car as a black Alfa-Romeo with license plate number 224WD53. Checking Tehran records —we found that the car actually belongs to you, Sulayman. Do you have any way of explaining the inaccuracy of this report?"

"No, sir; just off hand, I don't."

"Sulayman, it grieves me deeply, but I have to place you under arrest. It appears you have been complicit and an accomplice in the escape of a prisoner, and not just any prisoner, but the nation's prime prisoner, the Prime Minister of Israel."

Mamza Yasin places a call to Chief of Police Abbas.

"Chief Abbas, I have Sulayman Azzawi in my office. I am placing him under arrest for his part in the escape of the Prime Minister. Please send someone over to pick him up."

Chapter Twenty-Six

Friday – June 15, 2018

10:22 A.M. Sully has been brought into an interrogation room of the city jail. A Savama skilled interrogator is there to try to get some answers. Sully has been a senior member of Savama for the last twelve years, working as a mole for the CIA and, as such, knows all the tricks of the interrogation trade.

Savama agent Huda Muhsin begins, "Please tell me your name."

"My name is Sulayman Azzawi."

"How long have you been a member of Savama?"

"Twelve years!"

"Are you now or have you ever been a mole working for another country?"

"No!"

"If that is your correct answer, then why were you participating in the escape of a Harbush prisoner?"

"I wasn't!"

"Your car was seen speeding away from the scene of the prisoner escape."

"I have seen the area surrounding Harbush Prison many times over the years, and it contains many busy roads. And, over the years, I have traveled those roads many times which, as a matter of fact, was just recently."

"When were you last in the area of Harbush Prison?"

"Last Saturday!"

"What was your reason for going there?"

"I was meeting a friend."

"And your friend's name?"

"Salim Tilfah! Call him; he'll tell you I was there to see him."

"Oh, you can bet we will!"

"You know, Sulayman, I almost believe you, except for the bullet holes in your car."

Sully immediately recognizes this a trick question. *There is no way that anyone has had time to examine my car; plus, as I remember, Izzat only got off a couple of shots, and one of those hit the Prime Minister's shoulder.* "I have no idea what you are talking about. What kind of a trick question is that?"

"I just wanted to see your reaction, Sulayman. What do you know about the country's number one prisoner, the Prime Minister of Israel?"

What is he driving at now? "It appears I'm under arrest for allegedly aiding in the escape of this prisoner with no proof to back it up."

"Why do you suppose this prisoner was arrested in the first place?"

Here we go again! He's trying to catch me off guard to expose any possible hidden sympathies for Israel in connection with the Prime Minister's raid on Iran. "From what I have heard, he readily admits ordering the bombing raid on Iran's oil fields. Don't you feel that is reason enough?"

"Do you know what I think?"

"I haven't the slightest idea what you are thinking."

"I think you are doing a good job of evading the real issue of this interrogation, and you are going to tell me one way or another. Where is the Prime Minister?"

"How should I know where he is? I have no crystal ball!"

Agent Muhsin calls in a couple of officers and orders, "Cuff him and take him to the basement, then strap him to the chair."

Agent Muhsin then calls Director Yasin's office. "I've taken Sulayman to the basement. I'm getting nowhere being gentle. Send over Muzahim and Najim."

"Are you sure you want to go that route?"

"You want the location of the Prime Minister, don't you?"

"Yes, but go easy on him. He has befriended me a couple of times in the past."

Chapter Twenty-Seven

Wednesday – June 20, 2018

10:00 A.M. The courtroom is filled to capacity with a dozen or more standing in the rear. Azira is one of those standing in the rear. Like all cases involving only local citizens, the judge rules without trial and defense counsels and without a jury.

Sully is escorted into the courtroom with a guard on either side of him. He stands on a small platform with his hands in handcuffs behind him and shackles on his ankles.

The judge, dressed in civilian clothes, sitting behind his bench, addresses Sully. "Your name is Sulayman Azzawi?"

"Yes, it is!"

"I am told you have been a high ranking member of Savama Intelligence for a number of years. Is that true?"

"Yes, that is true; twelve years, to be exact."

"You are on trial here charged for aiding in the escape of a prisoner from Harbush Prison, and as I imagine you have been told before, not just any prisoner, but none other than the Prime Minister of Israel. What do you have to say regarding that charge?"

"I plead guilty, your Honor. I helped him escape. It was the right thing to do."

With that the courtroom bursts out with a roar with hoots and hollers. The judge pounds his gavel, ordering order in the courtroom.

After the courtroom quiets down, the judge again addresses the defendant, "So, you Sulayman Azzawi, plead guilty to the charge of aiding in the escape of the Prime Minister of Israel from Harbush Prison?"

"If you would like me to repeat it, yes, I plead guilty to the charge. I knew when I walked in here I would be found guilty regardless of whatever I said."

"I find your statement has a tone of contempt for this court."

"Are you going to fine me in contempt of court, your Honor?"

"I am tempted to! In all your years as a high ranking member of Savama, did you ever disclose any confidential information to the enemy?"

"Yes, I did; all the time. That was my job as a mole in the organization."

"I do not understand why you are so readily pleading guilty to everything?"

"As I said before, I knew my fate when I walked in here."

"If you know so much, Sulayman, you must know where the Prime Minister is now. Are you willing to tell the court of his location?"

"That, your Honor, I will not do."

"The court will go easy on you, if agree to disclose his location."

"I am not about to discredit my name and reputation by sinking that low."

"I feel there are ways of changing your mind."

"I have already experienced several days and nights of those ways, your Honor. The many blows and bruises that you see to my head are a testimony to that."

"In view of the fact, Sulayman, that you have plead guilty to aiding in the escape of prisoner, Prime Minister of Israel, and your confession to transmitting classified information to the enemy while acting as a mole inside Savama Iranian Intelligence, the court sentences you to death by hanging. Sentence is to be carried out at noon, one week from today in the Town Square. Case dismissed."

Sully is led out of the courtroom, back to the holding cell in the city jail, and Azira rushes back to the warehouse to give Roman, Rina, and the Prime Minster the sad news.

"One week from today, at noon, they intend to hang Sully in the Town Square."

Rina asks, "Why the Town Square? Why does it have to be so public?"

Roman responds, "That sentence is one man's justification of what the sentence should be. A death by hanging sentence will be reviewed by a higher authority and could very well be changed. I am sure the papers will keep everyone up to speed on this one."

Rina adds, "Well, if it is carried out as called, I plan on being there to give Sully some moral support."

Azira responds, "And you can count me in, too. I'm going to pay him a visit tonight."

Rina adds, "Count me in, too!"

• • • • •

7:13 P.M. Rina and Azira have both signed the visitors' log, only to be told that Sulayman Azzawi has been forbidden to see visitors. Hearing that news, Rina and Azira leave the police station almost in tears.

"Azira, Sully is sitting in that jail cell without the ability to see or talk to anyone. My national heritage may be Iranian, but right now, Azira, I'm not very proud of it. Let's head back to the warehouse."

DAY OF THE HANGING
Wednesday – June 27, 2018

The Town Square is filled to overflowing with tens of thousands of people, and it is so easy for anyone to get lost in the crowd. The gallows has been erected in the middle of the square, and the only person missing at the moment is Suiayman Azzawi. Roman, Rina, and Azira have taken a place close to the steps of the gallows hoping they will be close enough for Sully to recognize them.

• • • • •

11:45 A.M. The crowd is forced to make way for the police wagon carrying an impending martyr to the cause of justice in a nation of injustices. Still in shackles and handcuffs behind him, Sully is helped as he struggles to make his way to the gallows. As he almost reaches the stairs, he sees Roman, Rina and Azira there giving him a thumbs up. He smiles and nods to them as he begins the difficult climb to the top of the gallows. From there he is guided over to the trap door and the noose. He is asked if he has any last words.

"I lived my life for God and country!"

A black bag is pulled over his head, and then the noose is tightened around his neck. The executioner awaits the order. At the stroke of twelve, the order is given, and the trap door flies open. Not a sound is heard from anyone. The event is so rare that people leave the scene, stunned and overwhelmed by it all.

Roman, Rina, and Azira return to the warehouse completely overcome with the loss of Sully, a true friend and valiant soldier to the last, never revealing what he vowed never to reveal.

Azira remarks, "I have to get hold of Aaron Levy and have him pass on to Director Fred Graves at CIA that Sulayman Azzawi died a hero's death today. Rather than disclose the location of the Prime Minister, he made the ultimate sacrifice—death by hanging. He smiled and nodded as he passed us by, as if to say, 'All is well,' and with head held high, he boldly scaled those gallows' stairs, step by step to face and accept his dreadful demise."

Rina comments, "That news is going to come as a real shock to both Aaron and Fred Graves as Sully was a key player in Iran for a good number of years."

Rina then asks Roman, "What are your feelings about trying to make a break for it? It has been over two weeks."

"Sully's trial and death has been on the minds of too many people to try it just yet. Much as I hate to say it, I think we need to wait another two weeks. What do you think, Azira?"

"I think you are probably right. It wouldn't hurt. I have to feel they have done about all they can do in turning the city upside down, looking the Prime Minister. They may even feel he is out of the country by now."

"I'm sure they don't think that. If he were actually out of the country, that would be front page news in most every country in the world. How do you feel about it, Mister Prime Minister?"

"First of all, let me express my deep sorrow over the loss of Sully. He was a brave hero. I didn't know him very long, but I deeply miss him. He gave up his life for me rather than reveal where I was hiding. No man can do more than give up his life for another. Do you know if he has a widow?"

Roman responds, "I don't believe so. He worked for the CIA in the States, but as an agent, he spent his entire time here not exactly the best arrangement for a marriage."

"You asked me earlier how I felt about trying to make a break for it. You all have done a good job of keeping me alive so far; I rely on your good judgment."

"Okay, Azira, we'll wait two more weeks. Then we'll try the old delivery truck routine that worked so well before with Rina. Are you in good physical shape, Mister Prime Minister?"

"Roman, as I have mentioned before, please call me Ira, and yes, I feel I'm in good physical shape. Why do you ask, Roman?"

"The three of us will be hiding behind a large load of furniture in a truck taking us to the port of Now Shahr on the Caspian coast. It will probably be necessary to climb over this load of furniture."

"Oh, I see; well, I'll manage okay."

Chapter Twenty-Eight

Wednesday – July 4, 2018

9:36 A.M. Azira is sharing a cup of coffee with Roman, Rina, and the Prime Minister and goes on to say, "The papers lately have been reporting of Iran's determination to find the Prime Minister and their second attempt to go all out in this effort. I think we can expect another visit at some point, and next time, they may not stop with just opening one crate."

Rina remarks, "I was only known to be a fugitive on the run by Mahmud Abuzar, and he is no longer the Director of Savama Intelligence. I feel I am fairly safe to come and go in this town. I should be free to scout around and let you know if and when they are headed this way."

Roman responds, "I have a better idea. Rather than sitting here and hoping we can get away for some other place before being caught, I am going to surprise my aunt and uncle in town one more time and take advantage of their secret room in the basement. It's a room that my uncle built for his son Hasan when he decided he had enough of the Tehran police force and go on the run. As you remember, he died while on the run. I think we should make a run for it as soon as it gets dark tonight."

Rina adds, "I'm going with you and the Prime Minister tonight, just so I'll know where to reach you when the time is right."

"Good idea, Rina!"

•　•　•　•　•

9:29 P.M. Roman, the Prime Minister, and Rina are standing on the doorstep of Roman's aunt and uncle's home. Roman knocks on the door. They wait a minute or two. No one answers!

Roman mutters, "I hope they are home. I don't know where they would be at this time of night." Roman knocks again. Waiting another minute or two, Roman's uncle, Karim cracks open the door. "Uncle Karim, it's me, your nephew, Romahni Hawakhazi."

"Oh, Romahni! I can't believe it's you. Come in, come in! Maritza, it's Romahni!"

"Oh, Romahni, you're back. I can't believe it is really you. It is so good to see you again." Maritza runs over and gives Roman a big hug and kiss.

Then Roman points in the direction of the Prime Minister and says, "Maritza and Karim, I want you to meet a very special person that I have with me, and please do not be alarmed by what I am about to say. Standing here with me is the Prime Minister of Israel. I want you both to know that I regret deeply barging in on you like I have tonight. As you can imagine, this is not really a social call. Rina with me here and I have been given the mission of obtaining the Prime Minister's release from Iran. As you are probably aware, the Iranian authorities are looking high and low for him and for me, as well. I know I have put you both at risk. Please forgive me, but I have nowhere else to turn. Uncle Karim, your secret room in the basement worked so well before for me; could you please make room again for me and the Prime Minister?"

"Of course, Romahni, of course! You are family, and it is our honor to have such a very distinguished guest in our humble home as the Prime Minister of Israel."

Remaining quite silent up 'til now, the Prime Minister offers his hand to Karim and Maritza, adding, "I would like you to know that it is I who is deeply honored by your generosity. At the same time, I am hurt by putting you at risk like this,"

Karim responds, "Please, sir, don't give it another thought. You and Romahni will be perfectly safe down there, and Maritza and I are in no danger at all."

Rina, who has been standing aside up 'til now, runs over gives Roman a huge kiss and says, "It's time I say goodbye, everyone. Roman, I'll see you when the time is right." And Rina waves goodbye.

Maritza looks at Roman, and the Prime Minister asks, "Would you like something to eat or drink? I have some leftover apple pie and maybe a little milk."

Roman admits, "Right now that sounds great, Aunt Maritza! Ira, how about you?"

"I have to admit that sounds mighty good!"

The four of them sit down around the kitchen table while Roman and the Prime Minister are eating. Karim asks, "Romahni, where have you been staying up 'til now?"

"I really can't tell you too much. Right now, the less you know the better for you. But I can tell this much—Ira here and I both spent some time in Evin Prison, as well as Harbush Prison recently. How we managed to get out of both prisons is another whole story. Again, it is better if you didn't know."

Karim remarks, "Romahni, I don't know what you actually do for a living, but it sounds awfully dangerous to me."

"Rina, whom you just saw beside me a few minutes ago, and myself own a worldwide investigation firm in the United States that takes us to troubled spots all over the world. Recently we were called upon by Aaron Levy, the Director of the Mossad in Israel, to do what we could, to free the Prime Minister and bring him back to Israel. Being held captive in Iran seemed like an almost impossible task, but we agreed to do whatever it might take to get the job done. Sadly, the one person most instrumental in seeing that the Prime Minister got this far in his escape from Iran saw his life come to an abrupt end a week ago."

Karim asks, "Was that your friend who suffered that terrible death in the Town Square?"

"Yes, Karim, it was! He suffered a hero's death rather than betray another."

"Well, Romahni, we need to see what we can do to make you and the Prime Minister comfortable in your new home."

The Prime Minister interrupts by saying to Karim, "Please, Mister Hawakhazi, please call me Ira."

"Yes, sir, if you like!"

"Please, I would appreciate it."

The three descend the stairs to the basement. Then Karim asks Ira, "Look around and what do you see?"

"I see a very nicely wall paneled basement with a small bed, end table, and lamp."

"I'll show you something now you didn't see. Karim pushes on a side of the paneling and part of the paneling opens up with the aid of several blind hinges. There is a small handle on the reverse side of the panel to pull the panel closed once you are inside. The room is meant merely to hide someone on a temporary basis, but based on past experience, it does an excellent job of that. Romahni, you can sleep down here, and the Prime Minister…oh, I mean Ira can use the extra bedroom we have."

Ira interrupts by saying, "Please, I desire to sleep here in the basement. I am the reason for causing everyone so much trouble, and it is no trouble for me at all. Plus, if this home is suddenly interrupted by a search warrant, I will be automatically in the right place."

Karim comments, "I don't feel it right for the person who holds the highest office in the country to have to sleep in the basement. In the interests of harmony, Ira, I bow to your wishes."

Tuesday – July 10. 2018

3:18 P.M. Karim, Maritza, Roman, and the Prime Minister are gathered around the kitchen table, chatting and enjoying a cup of hot tea when they hear a knock on the front door. Karim motions to the Prime Minster, "Quickly, go to the basement and hide in your secret room. Don't make a sound and don't come out until I give you an all clear."

Maritza quickly clears the table of the extra place setting, and Karim walks slowly to the door and opens it. Two Tehran police officers address Karim: "We are sorry to bother you, sir, but we are conducting an all-out search of all buildings and residences in the city for a prisoner on the loose."

They show a picture of the Prime Minister to Karim and ask, "Have you ever seen this man?"

"That looks like a picture of the man that has been in the newspapers lately."

"I'm going to have to ask you to please step aside while we search your home, sir."

They look in all the closets, search under every bed, even glance in the rafters, and finally head for the basement. The only things visible to them are the small bed, end table, and lamp.

They turn to Karim, standing by, and ask, "This bed looks like it has been very recently used. Who uses the bed?"

"My nephew, Romahni, whom you saw upstairs with my wife."

"You have an extra bedroom; why doesn't he sleep there?"

"I know it may sound a little odd, but he says he likes sleeping down here because it is cooler."

Then one officer says to the other, "Come on, Mahmud; let's check this place off our list."

When Mahmud reaches the top of the stairs, he walks over to Roman and asks, "I understand you like to sleep in the basement when you could use the extra bedroom. Why do you do that?"

Roman quickly thinks, *This guy is trying to trap me into saying the wrong thing. What advantage does a basement have? It is generally cooler!* "I like sleeping down there because it is always cooler."

Mahmud comments, "Alright, Kahdr, I'm ready!"

In parting, Kahdr remarks, "Sorry to have troubled you. Goodbye!"

Karim waits five minutes before descending the stairs to the basement. "Alright, Ira, it's clear. You can come out now."

The Prime Minister cracks open the panel door and steps out.

Karim adds, "It was a little tense for a minute or two. One of the officers noticed the slept-in bed in the basement here. When I said it was used by my nephew, he questioned why he didn't use the extra bedroom. I had to quickly come up with a reason right then and there. The only thing I could think of right off hand was that he liked sleeping in the basement because it was cooler. Then, when this same officer reached the first floor, he made it a point to ask Roman why he liked sleeping in the basement. I was sweating little bullets wondering what Roman was going to say. I'm afraid he would have taken the wrong answer very seriously. Let's go back upstairs and join Roman and Maritza."

When they reach the top, the Prime Minister turns to Maritza and says, "I'm afraid I have been a terrible burden on you and Karim. Roman, isn't there any other place we can stay 'til that whole thing blows over?"

"I'm afraid not, sir!"

"Maybe we should try to make a break for it."

"I wouldn't recommend it, sir,"

"Didn't you say that they would hardly look behind a load of furniture?"

"Ordinarily, yes, but we are not experiencing ordinary times right now."

Chapter Twenty-Nine

Tuesday – July 31, 2018

2:26 P.M. Azira and Rina arrive in front of Karim and Maritza's home with their truck loaded with furniture. Azira gives a short beep on the horn, and Karim looks out the window.

Karim yells to Roman, "There's a large truck out in front honking its horn. Is it someone you know?"

"Yes, it is Azira Mahdi, and she, along with Rina, is telling us it is time to go. I know this is a little sudden, Karim, but Ira and I have to leave."

Roman runs into the kitchen and gives Maritza a big hug and kiss. "Aunt Maritza, it is time for Ira and me to go. You and Karim have been absolutely wonderful for hosting and taking care of Ira and me. We will never forget your kindness and generosity."

The Prime Minister shakes hands with Karim and Maritza, adding, "As Roman said, I will always remember your kind generosity for taking me into your home and saving my life. I will try to make it up to you in some way. Goodbye to you both and thank you so much!"

Roman and the Prime Minister wave goodbye as Azira opens up the rear doors to the truck and asks the Prime Minister to begin climbing over the huge pile of furniture. He is followed by Roman and then Rina.

Azira asks, "Are you all settled up front okay?"

They all yell back, "We're all set!"

"Try to relax and maybe get some shut-eye. It's going to be a long, four-hour drive."

After about an hour and a half, Azira comes to a halt. Roman hears some conversation taking place, and then the back doors of the truck are opened. A state police officer has stopped her truck to see what she is carrying. Roman touches his index finger to his lips signifying to keep quiet. At that very moment, the Prime Minister is doing his best to hold back a sneeze. Roman squeezes his nose, signifying to the Prime Minister to do the same. It worked!

Convinced that everything appeared to be in order, the police officer clears Azira to drive on.

As Azira pulls out and drives on, Roman mentions, "That stop we had must have been the normal check point at the city of Karaj. Which also means we are about one-third of the way to Now Shahr. We shouldn't have any more check points the rest of the way. Our biggest job when we get to Now Shahr will be making contact with Jasim while staying clear of the police. Unfortunately, I am too well known by the police in Now Shahr, Ira."

Roman laughs a bit, adding, "I'm afraid we have one other small complication; none of us has any money to pay Jasim for our boat trip to Baku. Iran was kind enough to help me unload my last rial when I was hauled into Tehran's city jail."

The Prime Minister claims he has no money, as well. Then Rina chimes in, "I have plenty of money. I was never arrested."

Then Roman laughingly remarks. "I knew there was a reason why I let you tag along on this trip."

"Ha! Ha! Very funny! You know darn well that you're no good without me!"

"You are so right, Rina, I really don't know what I would do without you!"

•   •   •   •   •

6:32 P.M. Azira's truck arrives at Now Shahr and parks along the wharf. She opens the rear doors and Rina begins crawling over the mass of furniture.

Roman and the Prime Minister remain inside for the moment, waiting to see what develops. Azira and Rina stand on the dock, looking out over the water to see if the Kutum Queat is one of the fishing boats about to moor alongside. After a few minutes, Rina remarks, "That looks like the Kutum Quest now." She starts waving, trying to get Jasim's attention. After a minute or two, Jasim sees Rina waving and waves back.

After twenty minutes or so, the Kutum Quest ties up alongside. Jasim disembarks as Rina and Azira run over to meet him.

Jasim asks, "Where's Roman?"

Rina responds by saying, "Jasim, I'd like you to meet Azira Mahdi. Azira was kind enough to bring Roman and the Prime Minister of Israel here in her truck."

Jasim extends his hand and says, "I'm very pleased to meet you, Azira. Perhaps you can tell me where Roman is?"

"Roman and the Prime Minister are still in the truck, waiting to see if the police arrive; you see they are both very wanted by the Iranian authorities. If the police knew they were both hiding in the truck, they would be arrested immediately. And speak of the devil, I see a police car now."

Officer al Sadi steps out of the car and walks over to talk to Jasim. "Jasim, what kind of a day did you have today?"

"It was a pretty good day. The crew is unloading the catch now."

"And who are these young ladies you have with you?"

Before Jasim has a chance to answer, Rina speaks up, "I am Latifa al Majid, and this is my friend, Azira Mahdi."

Officer al Sadi goes on to say, "I thought I knew everyone in Now Shahr, but I don't believe I have ever seen either of you before."

Azira responds, "Oh, we don't live here, officer; we are here to see our good friend, Jasim."

"Latifa al Majid! That name sounds somewhat familiar for some reason. Yes, now I remember we were looking for someone named Roman Hawk on Jasim's boat years ago. You and your husband had rented the boat for some kind of cruise. Where is your husband, Latifa?"

"He is visiting a friend on the outskirts of town and will be joining us later."

"And he left you here alone?"

"I'm not alone, officer; not with Jasim here."

"Does this truck here belong to either of you?"

Azira claims, "Yes, it is my truck, officer."

"Is it empty?"

"No!"

"What do you have in it?"

"Some furniture!"

"You are delivering a load of furniture at this time of day?"

"I'm not delivering it tonight, officer. It is loaded for delivery tomorrow."

Jasim finally speaks up, "Why are you asking so many questions, al Sadi? You are acting very suspicious of my friends!"

"I'm being paid to be suspicious. We've been told to keep an eye out for an escaped prisoner who might be trying to leave the country. Azira, let's take a look at what you have in your truck."

The doors are already open when they reach the rear of the truck.

"Why do you have the rear doors open?"

"Whenever I stop for any reason, I've always been in the habit of checking the load I'm carrying to see if it is still in good condition. It's just a habit I developed years ago."

"That would be a good place to hide, behind this load of furniture, but I'm not about to ask you to unload all that furniture. Some of those pieces look mighty, mighty heavy. I'm not sure I could lift them, and I know for sure you couldn't. Okay, Azira, I'm convinced. Close up your doors!"

Officer al Sadi begins walking back to his car, and looking back, yells, "You're a very lucky man, Jasim!"

Azira returns to Rina and Jasim. "That officer was very suspicious of our activity here, Rina. He even noted that taking shelter behind that load of furniture would be an ideal place to hide, but he readily admitted that unloading all that furniture was not a viable option."

Rina now turns to Jasim. "Jasim, Officer al Sadi had every right to be suspicious of Azira and me. You asked me a while ago where Roman was. Roman, who is wanted by the police, is hiding in the truck along with Iran's number one escaped prisoner, the Prime Minister of Israel. Roman and I were given the mission of obtaining his freedom and finding a way of sneaking him out of Iran. I know all too well Roman and I are asking a lot of you at this time, but we know you to be a good man that would be saving the leader of a country, the Prime Minister of Israel. You will never have an opportunity like this again in your lifetime."

"Undoubtedly, that is true, but at the same time, if and when Iranian authorities discover what I did, they will lock me up and throw away the key."

"Are you happy with the existing government?"

"I can't say that I am."

"What would think of turning your boat over to Samir if you decide to become an honorary citizen of Israel? You will be a national hero in that country, and I am sure the Prime Minister would fix you up with a brand new fishing boat."

"I can't leave my family here my wife and boy!"

"You can take them with you."

"I don't know Rina; I have to think about this."

"I think it's all clear now. Let's talk to the Prime Minister and get his input."

Rina looks at her watch and sees that it has been over a half an hour since Officer al Sadi left the scene. She gives one last look around the area, then she and Azira open the rear doors to the truck and yell inside, "Okay, you can come out now. It's all clear!"

Roman is the first to climb out. Four or five minutes later, the Prime Minister emerges, then the four meet with Jasim.

With tears in her eyes, Azira says, "I'm afraid it's time for me to say goodbye to you all. I don't know when I will see all of you again, if ever. I am going to miss you very much...especially you, Rina. I feel we formed a strong bond with the time we spent together."

Rina runs over and gives Azira a huge hug, and they give each other a little kiss on each other's cheek.

Rina says, "I will certainly miss you, too, Azira, but who knows, we could be back sooner than you think."

Roman shakes Azira's hand, saying, "You haven't seen the last of us, Azira. We'll be back before you know it, asking for your help again."

Finally, the Prime Minister says, "I never really got to know you as well as the others, Azira, but believe me when I say, I can't thank you enough for your kindness and generosity and putting up with me during my time in the warehouse."

"Mister Prime Minister, it was no trouble at all. It was an honor to help you." Azira now waves goodbye to everyone, hops into her truck, and gives a final wave as she drives off on the road back to Tehran.

Jasim then mentions, "Why don't we all go aboard the Kutum Quest, have a cup of Samir's good coffee and talk?"

They all agree, "That's an excellent idea, Jasim."

Once settled around the eating table, Rina leads off, "I was just telling Jasim a while ago about taking his wife and son with us to Baku. He feels strongly that he cannot aid in the escape of the Prime Minister without putting himself and his family in danger of being arrested. Hearing that I suggested that he take his family with him to Baku and that they travel on to Israel where he and his family will be national heroes. I even went on to say, Mister Prime Minister, that you would see that he received a brand new fishing boat as consolation for saving your life. I hope you'll forgive me, sir, for speaking for you."

The Prime Minister then speaks up, "I could not be more pleased to offer Jasim a brand new fishing boat, complete with all the gear and trimmings needed. We'll have a grand ceremony with every other fishing boat in the area, and you will meet them all, setting you up in business. I have yet to shake your hand, Jasim. My name is Ira Kaplan." They both shake hands.

"I am just Jasim to my friends."

Samir and three others were listening, just outside the cabin door. Samir cracks it open and says, "Please, take us with you, Jasim. None of us are really happy here!"

The Prime Minister remarks to Jasim. "Well Jasim, it looks like you will not only have a brand new fishing boat, but a ready-made crew to go with it. All we need is a word from you."

"You all have made it very difficult for me to say anything but yes. I think it all sounds too great to be true. I'll have my wife and son here at four tomorrow morning when we shove off. Thank you all, and especially you, Mister Prime Minister."

"No, thank you, Jasim!"

Chapter Thirty

Wednesday – August 1, 2018

4:00 A.M. Jasim needed no bell to wake the crew this particular morning. There is an air of jubilation in everyone's heart and mind realizing that they are leaving Iran and all its life stifling taxes, regulations, and police state tactics behind. The crew is laughing, joking, giving each other high fives, and anxious to get underway. For the first time ever, this will be no fishing trip. Jasim will be plotting a straight shot to Baku.

· · · · ·

4:22 A.M. Jasim walks aboard with his wife, Litzfa, and son, Jasim, Jr. Roman, Rina, and the Prime Minister are still asleep in the cabin. "Stow our things in the cabin, Litzfa, and then come back up on deck."

Litzfa stows what few things they were able to bring with them and returns on deck with Jasim and Jasim Jr.

"Well, Litzfa, we are starting a whole new life together. I know this has been rather sudden, and you are a little anxious about what lies ahead but try to look at it as a new and glorious adventure. We have an exciting life ahead of us, and we will be living in a country free to live as we please. Because of our part in freeing their Prime Minister, we will be welcomed with open arms.

I have been promised a brand new fishing boat, and the crew is anxious to leave the country and continue to be a team working together. So, you see, Litzfa, it was all meant to be!"

"I know, Jasim, you always know what is best. You have always been a good, faithful husband!"

The stirring in the cabin and on deck has aroused Roman, Rina, and the Prime Minister, and they join everyone up and about on deck.

Jasim gives the order, "Take in the stern line! Take in the bow line!" While hoisting sail, the crew starts singing an on old sea chantey, happy to be leaving port for a new land. Jasim takes the helm and plots a course due north. Roman, Jasim's son, and the Prime Minister join Jasim as Rina begins a conversation with Litzfa.

Rina begins to comment, "I know what must be going through your mind right now, Litzfa. The unknown of one's future can be a little frightening in a way, but believe me, you, your son, and Jasim have a wonderful future ahead of you. You see how happy and anxious the crew is to be leaving Iran. The Prime Minister has promised Jasim a whole new life, complete with a brand new fishing boat. And I know he will see that you are well received in Israel. You will have no trouble finding and attending a mosque of your choice. As for your son, the schools are the very best that you will find anywhere. So, you see, Litzfa, you really have nothing to worry about."

"You make it sound all so wonderful!"

"It will be, Litzfa, you'll see."

Roman comments to Jasim, "This seems like old times, Jasim; a little bit like our first trip, and on this trip, I won't have to be helping the crew pull in a net full of fish."

"Roman, I didn't ask you to take part in that."

"I know Jasim, I was just pulling your leg. I volunteered!"

"You were pulling my leg?"

"That's an expression that is sometimes used in America. It means, 'I was just joking' with you."

"Oh! Would either of you like to take the helm?"

The Prime Minister is the first to answer. "This will be an experience for me. Thanks, Jasim!"

"Hold a course of three forty-five!"

"Aye, aye, sir! Jasim, who is the three-hundred-pound monster in your crew?"

"That is Samir, the head crewman. He is totally loyal, and the one person nobody bothers to tangle with unless your name happens to be Rina."

"Are you talking about Roman's Rina?"

"Absolutely!"

"I don't think I understand. Are you inferring that Rina can in some way take on Samir?"

"I'm not inferring anything. I'll let Samir tell you."

Jasim calls over to Samir. "Tell the Prime Minister about the sparring round you had with Rina."

"Do I have to? It's embarrassing!"

The Prime Minister remarks, "My lips are sealed, Samir!"

"On the way to Now Shahr, Roman was telling Jasim that Rina could lick any man that would try to attack her. I told Roman that I didn't believe that and because of what I said, a match was set up to prove Roman's point. Although I thought the whole thing was rather silly and stupid, I agreed to do it. I really hate to say it, but Rina ended up throwing me overboard. Can you believe it? That little wisp of a thing threw me overboard. I climbed back on board with a new respect for that young lady."

Friday – July 3, 2018

10:28 A.M. Jasim places a call to the Baku harbor master: "My fishing boat, the Kutum Quest, is about two hours from landing. Please inform Israeli Ambassador in Azerbaijan that the Prime Minister of Israel is aboard. Ask him to pass on this information to Interim Prime Minister Kohl."

"You actually have the Prime Minister on board your boat? This is fantastic news. The whole world has to hear about this."

"I wouldn't make it public just yet. I'm still quite away offshore. Let's wait until the Prime Minister is actually on dry land, but please inform the Interim Prime Minister."

"I'll get on it right away." *The local operator won't know the phone number for Israel's Ambassador to Azerbaijan. I'll call the local newspaper. I'm sure they'll be able to give it to me.* "This is the harbor master calling. Can you give me the phone number of Israel's Ambassador to Azerbaijan?"

"Give me a minute. I'll look it up." A minute later, he says, "The number is 'AZ770529'. Why do you ask?"

"I really can't tell you, but it's hot!"

Two fishermen standing in the harbor master's office heard everything being said and left running out of the office.

The harbor master yells after them, "Where are you going?"

"No place in particular!" Ten minutes later, these same two fishermen burst into the office of the local T.V. station and start pounding on a counter to get somebody's attention. The person behind the counter turns around and yells to them, "Stop pounding on the counter. I can hear you. What is it?"

"We have some really hot news for you. We just came from the harbor master's office, and we heard him talking to someone coming into port about two hours away, claiming to have the Prime Minister of Israel on board and asking him to inform Israel's Ambassador. We thought the public ought to know of this terrific news."

"Thank you, gentlemen, for bringing this gigantic news to our attention. This is hot news!" The news editor is immediately notified.

He, in turn, contacts the producer of the existing show on the air and has a news broadcaster announce the following: "We are breaking into this broadcast to announce that this T.V. station has received alleged information claiming the Prime Minister of Israel is aboard a boat headed toward Baku, two hours away. You may recall that the Prime Minister was captured and taken prisoner by the authorities in Iran. If this information is true, this is an historic day for the nation of Israel. We now return to the program in progress."

Within minutes, the streets of Baku erupt with people shouting and congratulating the people of Israel. The harbor begins to fill with small boats headed out to sea to meet and greet the boat carrying the Prime Minister.

Israel's Ambassador to Azerbaijan calls Interim Prime Minister Kohl and he, in turn, notifies members of the Knesset, as well as Aaron Levy. The news on Baku's small T.V. station is suddenly captured on T.V. stations all over the world, including those of Iran. President Tahir al Majid is experiencing one of his daily fits hearing this news.

He calls Army General Zubaydi into his office. "The Prime Minister has managed to escape from Iran. He is believed to be on a boat two hours out of Baku. That is still in international waters. I don't want him reaching Baku. Send whatever many helicopters you need to intercept that boat and sink her, if necessary, but get the Prime Minister and bring him back here."

To assure his safe arrival, Azerbaijan sends out several military helicopters to greet the boat carrying the Prime Minister.

Jasim, Roman, and everyone on the boat are startled and surprised at the sight of the helicopters. Roman asks Jasim, "What do you suppose they are doing here?"

Jasim responds, "Your guess is as good as mine. No one is supposed to know we are inbound to Baku. I told the harbor master to keep the arrival of the Prime Minister quiet. He said he would!"

Roman comments, "I think maybe somehow the word got out. I'm also beginning to see a fleet of small boats on the horizon headed this way. I believe we are about to witness a welcoming committee."

Within a few minutes, the sound of fifty to a hundred boats honking their horns can be heard. The sound is almost deafening as they surround Jasim's fishing boat. Everyone in the small boats is joyously waving at Jasim's boat, and everyone on the boat is waving back. Then, in the distance, Roman sees a number of helicopters approaching from the south. "I don't like the looks of this, Jasim. Those helicopters could be ones from Iran and, if so, we could be in for a little trouble."

Within minutes, the Iranian helicopters are on the scene and begin firing on Jasim's boat. The Azerbaijan helicopters already on the scene begin firing back. After about two minutes of engagement, the Iranian helicopters back off. The commander opens up communication with his opposite commander of the Azerbaijan aircraft, saying, "Against the instructions of my President, I am returning to Iran. I do not want to be responsible for killing innocent civilians in all those small boats below. I will undoubtedly be serving some severe punishment for disobeying a Presidential direct order, but I won't have innocent blood on my hands."

As he heads back home, Azerbaijan helicopters wave back and forth from side to side in an attempt to wave goodbye to the Iranian commander. Within an hour, the Kutum Quest arrives at Baku's main dock, and Jasim gives his final orders from her, "Cast off the bow line! Cast off the stern line!"

As the Prime Minister disembarks the Kutum Quest, he is greeted by a host of individuals. The first person the Prime Minister sees is his wife Teresa. She runs over to him as he steps off the boat, and they hug one another as never before.

Next in line is Interim Prime Minister Kohl. They shake hands. "It is so good to see you back out of harm's way, Mister Prime Minister."

"Just call me Abram Kohl, sir. There is no Interim Prime Minister anymore."

The next person to shake the Prime Minister's hand is Aaron Levy. "You had a nation sitting on pins and needles all the time you were in Iran's hands. I sent Roman and Rina Hawk to Iran to somehow obtain your release. I see they were successful."

"It was a very costly mission, Aaron. We lost the life of a valiant soldier in CIA agent Sulayman Azzawi, but he was really better known to all as Sully. He was arrested by Iran authorities and put on trial. Rather than release my location to them, he suffered death by hanging. He gave up his life for me. I would like to hold a National Day of Prayer in his honor every June 27, the day of his death."

"I believe that will be a wonderful tribute to the man."

Last in line is Israeli's Ambassador to Azerbaijan. "I am most likely the least worthy in this line to shake your hand and tell you how happy we all are to see you back in safe hands."

All the while, the Prime Minister was greeted by his wife and dignitaries, flash bulbs were popping and T.V. cameras shooting this historic occasion.

But unknown to all at this moment, Azira has contacted the local paper in Tehran and leaked to them the story of how Izzat Zimam, notorious Commandant of Harbush Prison, bilked millions of rivals from prison funds by siphoning ten percent for his own amusement. A check of Bushehr bank records established it as fact.

Weeks later, the Tehran papers printed news articles about how former Warden and Commandant of Harbush Prison, Izzat Zimam, now chained in shackles, was last seen chopping wood a short distance from the prison he once commanded. With the latest change of command, the new guards appear to make no hesitation rebuking and goading Zimam as he chops down trees in a site just a short distance from the prison he once commanded.

"I can't wait to get back for our weekly hosing! Is today Friday?"

CPSIA information can be obtained
at www.ICGtesting.com
Printed in the USA
LVHW080240170321
681747LV00005B/19